FEMALE FURY!

She aimed the shotgun's yawning twin bores at Longarm.

"Get back on that horse and count your lucky stars, mister. You're the bastard killed my boy. He wasn't worth a bucket of warm spit, but he was my son. Next time I meet you with a Greener in my hand, I'll blow you in two. Now git, before I change my mind."

Longarm ran up the veranda steps and snatched the shotgun out of her hands. He broke open the weapon, dumped its loads out onto the ground, then closed the weapon and handed it back to her.

Descending the stairs, he said, "That's so you don't take it in your mind to shoot me in the back."

TABOR EVANS

LONGARM

AND THE
DEAD MAN'S BADGE

JOVE BOOKS, NEW YORK

LONGARM AND THE DEAD MAN'S BADGE

A Jove Book/published by arrangement
with the author

PRINTING HISTORY
Jove edition/December 1990

ISBN: 0-515-10472-8

Jove Books are published by The Berkley Publishing Group,
200 Madison Avenue, New York, New York 10016.
The name "Jove" and the "J" logo
are trademarks belonging to Jove Publications, Inc.

PRINTED IN THE UNITED STATES OF AMERICA

10 9 8 7 6 5 4 3 2 1

Chapter 1

It was a Monday morning and not raining for a change—which cheered Longarm up somewhat. Four days of a steady downpour had done much to clean the Mile High City's pungent air and tamp down the horseshit that filled the gutters and cobbled streets. Once again weary of his long, unwelcome hiatus in Denver, he hoped as he looked down at the narrow street below his window that the bright morning was a harbinger of more interesting days to come.

He left the window, padded stark naked across the threadbare carpet to his dresser, and peered at his reflection in the mirror. He had aroused himself with a whiskey-and-water whore's bath, after which he had shaved himself. He saw now that he had nicked himself on his chin. He swabbed it clean with the washcloth still damp from the alcohol and water. Staring back at him from the mirror was a satisfyingly big man, lean and muscular, with the hard body of a man who does not have time to linger over a meal. The flesh on his face lay tight over his cheekbones and chin, and had been cured to a saddle-leather brown by this big country's raw sun and razor-sharp winds. His eyes, narrowed to a squint from searching far horizons, were gunmetal blue, his close-cropped hair the color of aged tobacco leaf. A neatly trimmed longhorn mustache poised on his upper lip added a touch of ferocity to his lean, almost gaunt appearance.

He heard the rustle of bed sheets behind him, followed by the soft, light pad of bare feet, and turning quickly, opened his arms to pull close against him his fiery widow woman with the emerald eyes and the slash of pouting lips. Randy was as naked as he was, and had waited until she perceived that he had grown ready for her. Laughing with a deep-throated heartiness that shook the walls, Longarm kissed her on the mouth, swept her up in his arms, and carried her back to the bed, where he dumped her on her back. She was bouncing up, her thick shock of red hair flying, when he caught her under him. Prowling over her like a big delighted cat, he nailed her, relishing her sudden, tiny gasp of delight.

"Mmm," she whispered huskily.

2

Snaking her arms around his neck, she drew him hungrily down upon her.

Vail would just have to wait, Longarm told himself, as he closed his mouth over Randy's lush, pouting lips.

About an hour later Longarm glanced at his pocket watch as he passed the U.S. mint on the corner of Cherokee and Colfax. It was almost eleven. He would catch hell from Billy Vail, but then some things were worth being punished for, he commented to himself with a smile, his senses still faintly aware of Randy's perfume.

He turned the corner and started for the Federal Building just ahead of him. Once inside, he strode across the lobby through the swarms of officious, well-manicured, and barbered lawyers who filled the downstairs lobby. Ascending the marble stairs, Longarm strode down a short corridor to a large oak door. The gilt lettering on it read: UNITED STATES MARSHAL FIRST DISTRICT COURT OF COLORADO.

Longarm pushed the door open and entered the outer office. The clerk glanced up from his type-writing machine, a look of weary relief on his pink, beardless face.

"There you are, Mr. Long!"

"That's right, old son. You got the name right again. Chief in?"

"He certainly is," the clerk fairly sang. "He's been out here at least twenty times looking for you. He was thinking of sending me after you."

"You mean he's as hot as a cat's ass on a stove lid," Longarm suggested, leaning close to the clerk. "Is that it, old son?"

The clerk swallowed and pulled back anxiously, his momentary joy at Longarm's upcoming and well-deserved tongue-lashing fading from his pale cheeks. "Yessir, Mr. Long. The marshal is very anxious to see you. He just got a telegram this morning and he's been looking for you ever since."

"That so?"

"Yes, it is, Mr. Long. And I suggest you go right on in."

"You mean charge right on into the lion's den."

"Yes."

Longarm's big hand patted the clerk's tousled head; he straightened, swept on past the clerk's desk, and after a short knock on Vail's door, marched in. Billy Vail was pacing his small, cluttered office. He halted his pacing when he saw Longarm, his normally florid face even redder than usual.

"Where in hell you been, Longarm? You already missed the morning train."

"Was I supposed to be on it?"

"You sure as hell were!"

Longarm slumped into the red morocco-leather armchair and tipped his head slightly as he regarded his agitated superior. "Maybe you better start from the beginning, Billy."

Vail sat down in his swivel chair and peered unhappily at the clutter on his desk. Pushing aside a folder and a few opened letters, he snatched up a telegram and squinted down at it. Vail probably needed glasses, but what he needed even more was exercise. After half a lifetime of chasing outlaws, gunrunners, and assorted hardcases all the way to hell and back, he had been set down behind this desk and had promptly gone to seed; it was a fate Longarm vowed would never overtake him.

Brandishing the telegram, Vail looked across the desk at Longarm. "This here came in first thing this morning. It's from an old buddy of mine, Sheriff Dan Tompkins in Pine Hill, Wyoming. His deputy's bringing in that son of a bitch gave the local constable the slip last June after he was sentenced. You remember the bastard. Flem Cutter."

"Cutter? Yeah, I remember him."

"I figured you might."

What Vail was driving at was the circumstances surrounding Longarm's capture of Flem Cutter. When Longarm had gone to a local gin mill on Wykoop Street to collar Flem, the gunslick had started blasting away at him. His shots had gone wild as Longarm dove at him and cut him down, but one of Flem's errant shots had slammed into a kid running past the saloon. Luckily, the kid had survived the wound, but none of this had endeared Flem to Longarm or the local judge, who'd thrown the book at him. By all rights, Flem Cutter should now be languishing in Yuma prison.

"That's good news, Billy," Longarm said. "You want me to go up there after him?"

"Take the afternoon train."

Longarm got to his feet. "I'll pick up my travel vouchers and get my gear."

"When you reach Pine Hill, say hello to Dan Tompkins for me. He's seen a few years, but I hear he's still got a clear eye, and he's as honest as they come. That Cutter won't get loose from him."

"I hope not. See you, Billy."

"Keep your ass down, Custis. And get back here soon—or that widow woman'll have a fit."

Grinning, Longarm waved good-bye to Vail and left his office.

Swinging down from the train, Longarm walked along the platform to the baggage car, picked up his saddle, and went looking for a hotel. The selection in Pine Hill was not too choice, but he found what looked like a reasonably clean place, the Pine Hill Rest, and he entered the small but neat lobby. A round-faced clerk, sporting a green eye-shade and sleeve garters, looked up from behind the front desk. As Longarm dropped his saddle and carpetbag on the desk, the clerk opened the hotel register.

"A room for the night, mister?"

"No," Longarm said caustically. "I came in here to rent a horse. You mean to tell me this ain't the town's livery stable?"

"That's . . . that's down the street, mister."

Longarm gave up. "I'd like a room, old son. Sec-

6

ond floor and in back where it's quiet. If you got one."

The clerk reached back for a key and handed it to Longarm. "Number Twenty-two, mister."

Longarm signed the register. There was no bell-boy, so he lugged his gear up the stairs to his room, let himself in, and dumped his saddle in the corner. There was still plenty of light left in the day, he noted as he poured the water from the pitcher into the bowl and proceeded to wash the train's soot off his face and neck. A moment later he left the room to seek out some Maryland rye. His throat felt as dry as sandpaper.

He found the Maryland rye at The Drover's Home a few blocks down from the hotel. The place was crowded with noisy, unwashed patrons, over whom a burly barkeep—a powerfully built bull of a man—presided with unquestioned author-ity. He refused to fill Longarm's shot glass until Longarm paid for the drink. The price was at least ten cents more than Longarm was used to paying.

"Pretty steep, ain't it?" Longarm asked idly, slapping the coins down onto the bar.

"If you don't like it, mister," the bartender replied, sweeping the coins into his big palm, "you know what you can do about it."

Longarm took the shot glass over to a table against the wall and sat down with his back to it, his eyes on the batwings. He was anxious to check in with Sheriff Tompkins, and planned to do so as soon as he finished the rye. Meanwhile, he was hoping the sheriff might enter the saloon for a quick one. If he did so, Longarm could just as easily greet him here as in his office. A moment before, as Longarm walked down to the saloon, he had noticed the sheriff's office on the first floor of a frame building across from the jailhouse.

And then Longarm saw Meg O'Riley.

She was at least two hundred miles south of where he had last seen her, but there was no doubt it was she. The years had been kind to her, filling her out some, adding juicy heft to what had been a perfect figure to begin with. Longarm was that much older now to appreciate it. Her shiny black hair was piled high in the latest fashion, her red gown cut so low he doubted he would be able to see it when she sat down. She caught sight of him at about the same time his eyes found her, and he saw her brighten at once, her dark, magnificent eyes fairly glowing. After a quick word to the barkeep, she left the bar and moved swiftly across the sawdust floor to greet him.

When she reached his table, Longarm got to his feet and doffed his hat. Taking her hand gallantly in his, he brushed it lightly with his lips, a wide, mischievous grin on his face.

"There you go, Custis," Meg said, sitting down, "spoiling me all over again."

"You're some distance from Cheyenne, Meg. What in blazes are you doing in this town?"

"Working—as usual. I own the place, Custis, me and my husband."

"Your husband?"

"The bartender. Bull Danham."

"He's your husband?"

"Now don't let that hold you back none, Custis. He don't matter worth a pinch of coon's shit. And you know what happens when the two of us get together."

"We begin to smoke."

She laughed. "And then we singe together."

"But I don't want to cuckold that little ol' feller. He looks like he knows how to hold a grudge."

"And then some. But it ain't that way between us, Custis. Me marryin' him was just a business deal. I needed him to get a license—and he does manage to keep the customers from damaging the furniture."

"And he doesn't get any of your trade for his troubles?"

"It would be churlish of me to hold back, don't you think, Custis?"

"Yes, I do. So, if you don't mind, I'll pass on this one."

Her eyes flashed angrily. "You do, and maybe I'll cause trouble. I want you, Custis—and I know you want me."

"Right now, all I want is to the see the sheriff. Pick up a bravo he's got in custody and take him back to Denver."

"You can't take him with you anywhere tonight. There's no train out. So come back here after you see the sheriff. Hear?"

He grinned at her and shrugged his shoulders. "I hear."

As he got up to go, she reached up and took his arm just above the elbow and drew him closer. "It's good to see you again, Custis. I really mean that."

He patted her hand and gently pulled free. "It's good to see you again too, Meg."

"You come right back now. Hear?"

"I hear."

He clapped on his hat and left the saloon.

The sheriff's office was open, but the sheriff was not in it, even though the lantern on his desk was lit. Longarm left the office and crossed the street to the jail. He was just mounting the short flight of cement steps when the explosion that ripped out the jail's backside detonated. The jail's door went sailing toward Longarm, while the force of the blast sent Longarm flying back into the street; the door cartwheeled crazily past him as he landed hard on his back, his head slamming to the ground. He fought to keep himself conscious while he rolled onto his stomach and folded his arms over his head to protect it from the chunks of brick, steel bars, and a wild assortment of debris that rained down upon him.

As soon as the lethal barrage ended, Longarm jumped up. A dark pall of smoke and debris was just lifting, revealing a gaping hole where the jail's roof had been. A major portion of the front wall had been swept away and he was able to see—through the jail's twisted cell bars—the outhouse in the alley behind the jail. It was leaning dangerously back off its foundation. At the same time he heard the distant pounding of fading hoofbeats as those who had just attempted to blast a prisoner free made their escape.

Longarm ran up the still-intact steps of the jailhouse, aware of a noisy, excited crowd charging down the street toward the jail. Picking his way over a beam, he walked up to an overturned desk and, looking behind it, found himself staring at the remains of a white-haired man crumpled on the floor. The star pinned to his vest was clearly visible. One quick look at the back of the man's shattered skull where it had smashed into the wall and Longarm knew he had come too late to pay his respects to Sheriff Dan Tompkins.

He stepped over the rubble into the cell block and saw the prisoner those damn fools had come to free. His charred and blasted remains were all that was left of him. Part of him was wrapped around a bar, but not much, and Longarm had to look closely in the wreckage of his cell to see where the rest of his head had gone. After a grisly, stomach-twisting moment, Longarm gave up looking.

The smell of cordite hung heavy in the ruins. What had happened, Longarm figured, was the outlaws, more used to black powder than this new-fangled dynamite, had overestimated the amount it would take to break through the jailhouse wall and had blown up the entire jail instead.

A rough hand grabbed Longarm's arm and flung him around. Longarm found himself looking into

11

the swarthy, unshaven face of a man wearing a deputy's badge.

"Who're you, mister? Where'd you come from?"

"I might ask you the same thing," Longarm told him, yanking free of the man's grasp. He took out his wallet, flashed his deputy marshal's badge. "Name's Custis Long. I'm here to take back that fugitive you just brought in."

"Flem Cutter?"

"He's the one you brought in, ain't it?"

"Oh . . . yeah, sure. I'm Seth Turrell."

"You better take a look at your sheriff, deputy. He's over there under that desk."

Turrell followed Longarm's gaze. "Oh, Christ," he said.

Another deputy, judging from the star on his vest, charged into the wrecked jail. With an angry curse, he flung aside the desktop and knelt beside the dead sheriff. After a quick check, he slowly took off his coat and dropped it over the man's face. Then he looked over at Turrell.

"What about Cutter? Did them bastards free him?"

"I don't know, Cal."

"Well, find out, dammit!"

Turrell brushed past Longarm and picked his way hastily into the shattered cell block; he returned a moment later, his face ashen.

"You better not go in there, Cal," Turrell warned him. "The poor bastard's still in there, all right. But only a part of him. It sure as hell ain't very pretty."

12

By this time the crowd that had gathered was pushing up into the jailhouse, eyes wide with excitement. Longarm pushed out past them and went looking for The Drover's Home and Meg O'Riley.

He needed a drink bad—and maybe Meg O'Riley's comfort to go with it.

Chapter 2

"I'm real sorry you lost that fugitive you were after," Meg said, pulling her beer stein closer and taking a sip of the beer.

The saloon was beginning to fill up again, the entering townsmen filling the place with their excited buzz as they joined the crush at the bar.

"I should be thinking good riddance," Longarm said, leaning back in his chair. "But somehow, after seeing what that dynamite did to Cutter, I haven't got the heart for it."

Meg shook her head unhappily. "We're all goin' to miss Dan. He would've had no trouble at all getting re-elected. Now it looks like a shoo-in for Levinson and his crowd."

"Levinson? Who's he?"

"He owns the Cattleman's Rest down the street. He's a big man in town, head of the county council, and he's after the sheriff's job. He didn't have a chance while Dan was alive, but he'll make his move now. You can bet on it."

Longarm thought that over. Every cloud had a silver lining—at least this one had for Levinson. Interesting. Perhaps.

"You'll be goin' back now?" Meg asked.

He felt as always Meg's vital, animal warmth, and it brought back pleasant memories. He shrugged regretfully. "No reason for me to stay, Meg. I guess I'll be taking the train out tomorrow."

"Well, at least that gives us tonight."

"It does at that."

A staggering, unshaven imitation of a ranch hand approached their table. The weight of his sixgun dragged his cartridge belt down past his thighbone. His Levi's, shirt, and vest were filthy, the red bandanna around his neck encrusted with dried sweat and dirt. Only one of the man's spurs was functional, and his flat-brimmed hat rested on his back, suspended by its cord, revealing a shaggy growth of unkempt hair that hid his ears completely, along with most of his forehead. Someone had crushed his nose in a fight and the mean, feral eyes that now peered at the two of them reminded Longarm of the eyes of a wild pig he had come upon once in a box canyon.

The moment Meg saw him approaching, she shrank back in her chair. Behind this shaggy apparition came Meg's husband and business partner, a sawed-off cue stick in his hand, his face dark with grim purpose. Evidently Bull knew this gunslick was about to cause a ruckus and was getting ready to nip his revolution in the bud.

Longarm pushed himself a little way out from the table and unbuttoned his frock coat to give himself easier access to the .44–40 double-action Colt resting in his cross-draw rig on his left hip. But as the gunslick came to a halt beside the table, he paid no heed to Longarm, concentrating his furious gaze on Meg.

"You ain't busy with this gent, Meg," he told her.

"What're you tryin' to say, Slope? 'Course I am."

"No, you ain't. It's my turn."

"Your turn?"

"We got business together upstairs."

"You foul pig," Meg spat, her voice shaking with fury. "I ain't got no business with you, Slope— ever."

"Hey, Meg, that ain't the way you talked in Cheyenne. Whatsa matter? You got religion all of a sudden?"

"Get out of here!"

"Hell, no. We're goin' upstairs."

As he reached for Meg's arm, Bull Danham swung around in front of him and pushed Slope violently back, then raised the cue stick threateningly. Blinking, a flash of amused contempt in his expression, Slope steadied himself and fixed his eyes on the bartender.

"Put down that toothpick, Bull," he said. "It won't do you no good now. This here's a new town. Ain't you heard? Dan Tompkins is a dead man."

"I don't care," said Bull. "Just keep your hands off my wife."

"Your partner, you mean. She ain't no wife of yours."

As he spoke, Slope lurched forward again, clumsily brushing Bull aside. Furious, Bull brought down his cue stick. But Slope warded off the blow with a quick upward stroke of his left hand and with his other yanked the cue stick out of Bull's hand. Swinging it back at Bull, he caught him on the side of his head and sent him reeling backward into a table. The table tipped under his weight and he went down, barely conscious, amidst a wreckage of beer glasses and broken chairs.

Turning back to Meg then, Slope reached down and grabbed her wrist.

Longarm stepped away from the table. "Let her go, Slope."

"You telling me what to do, mister?"

"Let her go."

"This here's a lovers' quarrel, mister. Stay out of it."

Longarm took another step away from the table. "Not likely."

Slope swore and flung Meg aside and drew his sixgun, all in one motion. Before Slope could fire, Longarm rammed a table into Slope's gut, driving

18

him swiftly back into the wall, pinching his gun hand between it and the edge of the table.

Slope grabbed the edge of the table, flung it aside, and charged Longarm. The two met like two grizzlies fighting over a female in heat, and in a moment they were rolling on the floor, entangled, punching, and clawing at each other. Somehow Slope managed to fight himself free of Longarm's grasp, and kicking out at Longarm, caught the lawman behind his right ear.

Stunned, Longarm took a moment to clear his head, then found himself staring up into the bore of Slope's cocked sixgun. As Slope's finger tightened on the trigger, Longarm flung himself to one side. The powerful detonation filled the saloon. The slug slammed into the floor just behind Longarm. Sawdust sprayed into the air. Longarm kept on rolling, palming the derringer in his vest pocket, hit the wall, then sat up to see Slope grinning down at him as he took a more careful aim.

Shouts came from all sides telling Slope to put down the gun, but only Meg made any effort to stop him. Flinging herself on him like a wildcat, she punched and clawed at his face, attempting to gouge his eyes out. But she was no match for Slope. He sent her reeling with a contemptuous shove.

Which gave Longarm no choice.

He emptied both of his derringer's barrels at Slope. The .44-caliber slugs made neat holes in Slope's filthy shirt just above his sagging cartridge belt. Slope dropped his gun and staggered back stupidly, then sat down on the floor, both hands trying to stem the mess pulsing out of his gut, his astonished eyes focusing on the dark, evil-looking flow of blood that pumped inexorably through his fingers.

"Jesus," he said, staring around him at the transfixed spectators, who were now crowding close around him, their faces ashen. "I'm gutshot!"

"Get Doc!" someone cried.

"Put him up on the bar," Bull said. He looked groggy but was on his feet once more. "The doc can work on him there."

Longarm stood up, recovered his .44-40, and dropped it into his cross-draw rig, angry with himself for letting this unpleasantness go so far. He wished he had not had to shoot the man.

"Custis, you all right?" Meg was standing beside him, concern on her face.

"I'm fine, Meg. How about you?"

"Never mind that. Let's get the hell out of this."

"Why the hurry?"

"Dammit, Custis. Don't argue with me. Do you know who this guy is?"

"No, and I don't much care."

"Brian Levinson's half brother. And right now Levinson is the law in this town."

"What about Seth Turrell?"

"He's no match for Levinson. No one in this town is—not now, not with Dan Tompkins gone."

"I shot Slope in self-defense. You saw that and so did everyone else in the saloon."

"Please, Custis! Come with me. I have my own private apartment upstairs."

Longarm smiled down at her. "After the way you took on that fool, I guess I got no right to protest. Lead on, woman."

As they threaded their way through the crowded saloon, Longarm looked toward the bar and saw four men lifting Slope onto it. A black trail followed the four men across the sawdust-covered floor. The blood was gouting from the dying man's gut with the force of an open spigot.

Meg pushed through a door leading to a stairway, Longarm on her heels.

Once in Meg's apartment, Longarm walked over to the window and looked down at the crowd in the street milling in front of the saloon. Further down he could see the shell of the jail, thin traces of smoke still rising from it. His gaze continued on across the street to the sheriff's office. Too bad Sheriff Tompkins hadn't remained inside there. And where had those other two been?

Meg moved up beside him, leaning her head against his shoulder.

"What a terrible day," she said to Longarm.

"And it's not over yet."

"I know."

Troubled by more than he could rightly put a finger on, Longarm turned from the window and looked down into Meg's face.

She saw the look in his eyes. "What's wrong, Custis?"

"There's not much in this that rings true, Meg. Something's going on around here I don't understand. I came up here to bring back Flem Cutter, a fugitive Dan Tompkins's deputy was bringing in. A simple enough assignment. Now both the sheriff and Flem Cutter are dead, and I end up gut-shooting that no-account downstairs."

"And now you're up here alone with an old flame."

He grinned. "Yeah. But don't distract me, Meg. What's goin' on around here, anyway?"

She shrugged. "It's election time. That usually brings out the worst in everybody. I saw it happen in Cheyenne."

"What's up for grabs?"

"The sheriff's job."

"And this Brian Levinson is running for county sheriff?"

"Yes, Custis, and now he won't have any opposition."

"I gather that's not so good."

"I don't think it is, and quite a few agree with me. Not that any of them would dare speak up now."

"Why do you say that?"

Meg frowned, turned, walked over to the bed, and sat down on it, clasping her hands in her lap. "It's all talk, Custis. But it boils down to the fact that no one really trusts Levinson. He's a very ambitious man. Too ambitious."

"Ambitious men are sometimes dangerous."

"Yes. Levinson has a big ranch outside of town,

and his crew is made up of hard, mean men—
hardcases like Slope, some a lot worse."

"And now—with Sheriff Dan Tompkins dead—
Levinson has a clear shot at the job of county sheriff."

"I don't see how anyone can stop him. The election's in less than a week."

"And no one will dare run against him."

"Not anyone who prizes his scalp."

Longarm left the window and approached the
bed. As he did so, Meg got to her feet, moved close
to him, and flung her arms about his neck. "Wipe
off that frown, Custis. And let's talk about something else."

"Better still," Longarm said with a grin, "let's
not talk at all."

She moved closer, went up on tiptoes, and kissed
him full on the lips, then stepped back and peeled
off his brown tweed jacket, after which she helped
him slip off his vest.

"I'm sure glad you still carry that cute little
derringer," she said, hefting the vest a couple
of times before draping it over the bed's corner
post.

Longarm slipped out of his cross-draw rig and
draped his .44–40, double-action over the same
bedpost. Meg's fingers fairly flew then as she dis-
robed, then helped Longarm peel out of his boots
and britches. Before long they were on top of the
bedspread, as naked as jay birds.

As his big hand swallowed her breast, he muttered huskily, "This has been a long day for me,

Meg. Maybe I can't do my duty for you as a gentleman should."

"Now don't you worry none about that, Custis."

Her hand snaked down between his legs and took hold of him. At once he felt himself quicken, his loins tingle. Laughing softly, she pressed closer. "See? You're not that tired. I hear tell a woman in heat can revive the dead. If she has a mind to, that is."

Longarm clasped her to him; their tongues entwined. Moaning softly, she thrust herself still closer, then pulled her lips away from his and bit his shoulder. It was just a tiny bite, after which she kissed the hurt away. He felt the moist heat of her tongue sliding along the slope of his shoulders to the strong cords of his neck, where she nipped him again. This time he cried out, then kissed her on the nape of her neck while she nibbled delightfully on his earlobes. Pulling her lips from his ear, she kissed him again—passionately, her tongue darting, her long, scented hair spilling over Longarm's shoulders.

He was fully alive now and ready for her, his pulse quickening. A searing lance of desire swept up from his loins. Pulling away from her flaming tongue, he hauled her over onto him, his massive erection disappearing with effortless ease into her muff's lovely sweet warmth. It was her turn to laugh now as she flung herself back and down, grinding his erection deep into her, seemingly bent on swallowing him entirely. He grasped her hips and started rotating her fiercely. As they built surely to a climax, she flung herself forward onto his chest, her tongue pressing boldly, wantonly past his lips and deep into his mouth to embrace his own tongue—a wild, passionate counterpart to his own thrusting erection.

That did it. He clasped both arms around the small of her back, lifted himself under her—and came to a shuddering climax. As his lips clung to hers, he felt her uncontrolled pulsing as she too reached her climax. More than once she came, each time crying out in her passion—while he kept his mouth firmly clasped on hers until, at last, completely satiated, she sank limply forward onto his long frame. Sighing, she kissed him slowly, tenderly, then rested her cheek on his chest.

"Mmmm," she murmured, "that was nice. So nice. Like old times."

Longarm stroked her long dark tresses and said nothing.

"You'll be going back to Denver tomorrow?" she asked.

"I'm not sure."

"But that man you came for is dead."

"And so is the sheriff. It stinks, Meg. I think maybe I should hang around a while longer and look into the botched jailbreak."

"Ah," Meg said, bending close and kissing him lingeringly on the lips. "I'm glad. It'll be fun waking you up—like I used to."

Longarm chuckled, then closed his eyes. The last thing he remembered before dropping off was

Meg struggling to pull the coverlet and sheets out from under his long body, then tucking him in.

It was the next morning when Brian Levinson pulled his buggy to a halt and tied the reins around the brake handle, his eyes studying the grim group of gunslicks waiting for him on the big house's veranda.

As he stepped down out of the buggy, his contemptuous glance swept over them. "What're you men doin' standing around for? Ain't you got nothin' better to do?"

"Sure, Boss," said Sim Bond, his foreman, "but . . . we got something to tell you."

"Yeah, I heard," Levinson said, grinning. Close to forty, he was a tall, powerfully built man, with a face resembling cured leather, a powerful hook of a nose, and a solid chin. Only the eyes, uncertain, forever shifting, betrayed his inner uncertainty. "Some gang tried to break that criminal loose and blew up him and the sheriff."

"That ain't what we mean, Boss."

On the veranda steps, Levinson pulled up. "Well?"

"It's your brother."

"Slope? What about him?"

"He's . . . dead, Mr. Levinson."

Levinson looked quickly about at the grim faces of the other men, then back at Sim Bond. "What do you mean, dead? What happened?"

"A deputy marshal come for that prisoner gut-shot him."

Levinson said nothing, but his face grew some-what paler, his dark brown eyes a little more bleak.

"There wasn't nothing the doc could do," Sim went on. "He died in The Drover's Home, on top of the bar."

"What the hell happened? What was he doin' in there?"

"He was after Meg. But this U.S. marshal cut him down. Used a belly gun."

"Does Ma know?"

"We thought it'd be better if you told her, Mr. Levinson."

"Yeah. Okay. Thanks, Sim. You men can go on about your business now."

Sim Bond, Lundstrom, and the five others trailed off the porch. Levinson held up in the doorway to watch them go, wondering why in hell they were so somber. Wasn't a single one of them cared a stick for Slope. Fact is, they should be in town celebrating.

He turned about and pushed into the house. The Indian housekeeper approached. She was as big and wide as a rainbarrel, her shiny black hair braided into two ropes riding her enormous breasts.

"Coffee, and some doughnuts, Carlotta—if you got any fresh made."

The Indian pulled to a stop, nodded impassive-ly, and turned to slipper back down the hall to the kitchen.

Brian turned into the huge living room and

found his mother in her usual spot by the window that gave her a view of the north pasture and the dirt road winding through the hills toward the ranch. She was in a wheelchair, an Indian blanket over her lap, a basket of knitting on the floor beside her. She turned her chair with knobby, arthritic hands and watched him approach, her cold, disapproving gaze boring into him.

Someday, just once, he wished she'd smile when she saw him. Like his pa used to do. The welcome in his old man's eyes had always been there, a reflection of his pride and love. From this woman he got only sullen, bleak pronouncements about his inevitable weaknesses, his countless shortcomings—even though she'd have nothing, only a cruel poverty and death, if he hadn't worked and schemed so hard to give her this great old house and provide her with the wealth to run it.

He bent to kiss her wrinkled parchment of a cheek, which as usual she proffered instead of her lips, then slumped down in the sofa next to her, his usual spot whenever he came into this room—which was not all that often.

"It worked," he told her. "Sheriff Dan Tompkins won't be running for sheriff next week."

Her pale eyes lit with the news. She had never liked Dan Tompkins, which meant he wouldn't have to go into any details. She wouldn't be interested.

"There's other news too," he said.

She pursed her lips and waited.

"I just heard it a few minutes ago. Out there on

the veranda. The men just told me."

"Told you what?" Her voice was as sharp as an icicle.

"Slope's dead."

Turning her head to gaze out the window, she said nothing. Brian watched her closely. Slope was her son by a husband she had left before marrying Brian's father. She had not taken the boy with her when she left, so appalled had she been by his behavior. But Slope had shown up three years ago. Her real punishment had begun then as she was forced to witness Slope's brutal, casual depravity. Watching Slope himself, Brian had come to understand why his mother had left her first husband. Slope, his mother had told him in a rare confidence, had turned out to be exactly like his father, as long before she had known he would.

Her relentless eyes still looking out the window, she said, "I regard this as a deliverance."

"Don't you want to know how it happened?"

"I presume it was a violent death, provoked by his lusts. An enraged husband, perhaps?"

"He got in a fight with a marshal and was shot in the gut."

"Over a woman, I presume."

"Meg O'Riley."

"That tart runs The Drover's Home?"

"Yes."

She turned in her wheelchair to look at him. "Bury him somewhere on the ranch. Don't tell me where. And I don't want any marker."

29

He looked close to make sure she was serious. There was not a single tear in her eyes, and one look into those cold, implacable eyes and he knew she had meant every word.

"All right. I'll take care of it."

"This marshal. You know anything about him?"

"I just heard about this a few minutes ago. How would I know anything about him?"

"You going to let this marshal get away with killing my boy?"

"Hell, no."

She looked back out the window, a single tear rolling down her cheek. "Good," she said. "Make sure you don't."

Brian got up from the sofa, as always, his mind struggling to fathom his mother's cold, inscrutable nature. One thing he knew for certain, however. She'd meant what she'd just said, so he'd better not let that son of a bitch of a marshal walk away from what he'd done.

As he reached the doorway, her cold voice startled him. "And don't forget about that tart either."

He continued across the hallway into his room. The housekeeper had left his coffee and doughnuts on the small round table beside his bed. He took off his hat and flung it onto his bed, and sat down in the captain's chair he'd covered with a buffalo robe. He picked up a doughnut and pulled the coffee toward him.

Sipping the hot coffee, he found himself contemplating the unpleasant job he had before him—several, in fact—and realized wearily that for a while he wasn't going to have much of a chance to take it easy. This galled him, especially after solidifying his deal with Cyrus Gurney and after the way he'd settled Sheriff Dan Tompkins's hash. By all rights he should have been settling back with a smile, contemplating the clear road ahead.

Now he was facing an early start the next day, well before dawn. No rest for the wicked.

Chapter 3

A construction crew was already clearing away the jailhouse's debris as they got ready to rebuild it when Longarm entered the sheriff's office. The two deputies were sitting quietly in the office, Seth Turrell on the bench under the gun rack, Cal behind the sheriff's desk.

"Morning, gents," Longarm said.

Seth simply nodded.

Cal said, "Good morning, Marshal. Looks like you came a long way for nothing."

"It does, at that. Sorry about the sheriff, not so much about the prisoner. He was a mean one."

"Yeah," said Seth. "He sure was."

"You the one brought him in?" Longarm asked Seth.

"That's right. I brought him in."

"You sure you got the right man?"

Seth pulled back, immediately on the defensive. "What're you sayin', Marshal? Of course I got the right man."

"Chunky fellow, was he?"

"Yeah. That's right."

"Kinda slow-talking, easygoing."

"He talked kinda slow, sure. When he saw I had him cold, he gave up and came along without no trouble."

"How'd you find him?"

"We got a tip from Sim Bond. Said he was hidin' out in the hills."

"Sim Bond?"

"He's the Jinglebob foreman."

"Jinglebob?"

Cal spoke up then. "A ranch nearby, about ten miles out. Biggest one in the valley."

"So when the sheriff got word Cutter was out there, he sent you after him. That the way it was, Seth?"

"Yeah. That's the way it was."

Longarm looked from one man to the other. "What I'm wonderin' is why the sheriff wasn't over here in his office when that gang blew up the jail."

"We was up the street, real busy."

"Busy?"

"That fellow you ventilated last night," Cal said.

"Slope?"

"Yep. He was causing a ruckus in the barbershop; then he threw some food around in the restaurant. I had to go down there and help settle him down. Seth here was in trouble and needed help."

"You two didn't do a very good job."

"He promised to mend his ways."

"What could we do?" Seth said, breaking in. "We thought he was drunk and disorderly. But he wasn't drunk—and the argument in the restaurant turned out to be only a misunderstanding."

"Some misunderstanding. He was ugly enough when he went after Meg O'Riley."

"That was later."

"So while you two were off quieting Slope down, the sheriff was left in the jailhouse."

"That's what happened, all right," said Cal, his face drawn. "I sure as hell wish he'd stayed over here."

"Turned out to be a fatal mistake," Longarm said.

The two deputies just looked at each other, then away. They seemed as depressed as Longarm at what had happened. Or maybe they were just two very good actors. Longarm walked back to the office doorway and looked across the wide street at the demolished jail.

His mind was racing. He knew now that the sheriff's death had not been accidental. He had been murdered. But there was no proof Longarm could present to a jury. Only a series of unfortunate coincidences—and the fact that the man they

35

had arrested and jailed as Flem Cutter was not, in fact, Cutter. Cutter was not a chunky, easygoing fellow under any circumstances. He was a lean, gangling, lantern-jawed wild man with fire in his eyes, as easy to hold on to as a greased eel, as likely to bite a lawman as go quietly. And if that was Cutter's gang who'd tried to bust him out, where in hell did they come from? Cutter was too mean ever to run with a gang—and too smart as well. He was a mean loner who would have found it impossible to take direction from the Devil himself.

Longarm turned back to the two deputies. "You say the one who first sighted Cutter was the Jinglebob foreman?"

"That's what I said," Seth replied.

"Who owns the Jinglebob?"

"Brian Levinson."

"Yeah," chimed in Cal. "Him and his ma."

"I might like to ride out to the Jinglebob," Longarm said. "How would I get there?"

"North of town's a trace heading west," Cal told him. "Follow it for about ten miles and you'll see the big house."

"Can't miss it," said Seth.

"Only I wouldn't go out there, not right now," said Cal.

"Why not?"

"Slope was Brian Levinson's half-brother."

"I know that."

"Brian Levinson is very polite, Marshal. A gentleman. And a very influential man in this town.

36

From the look of things, he's going to be our new sheriff. But that don't mean he don't know how to hold a grudge."

"Him and his ma," said Seth.

"Thanks for the warning."

Longarm left the sheriff's office and headed down the street to the livery.

The Jinglebob's big ranch house was impressive. It sat on the side of a hill under a crown of oaks. The barns, work sheds, bunkhouse, and cookshack were a well-planned distance away, the big trees shading them all. The house was painted white, and had a veranda running across its front. Longarm was following a rutted trace, and as he rode closer to the ranch, the sun resting heavily on his shoulders, he found himself looking forward to the cool shade of those ten or more trees towering protectively over the Jinglebob compound.

Entering the compound, he nosed his mount over to the big house, dismounted, and flipped his reins over the hitch rack in front of it. He was about to mount the veranda steps when an old woman in a wheelchair appeared in the doorway, a wide-bottomed Indian housekeeper holding open the door. Her gnarled hands pumping on the wheels, the woman guided herself smoothly out onto the veranda. In her lap was a double-barreled shotgun, which she promptly leveled on Longarm.

"And just where might you be goin', mister?"

"I'd like to speak to Sim Bond."

37

"Half of this spread is mine. You can talk to me. What do you want with my foreman? You got two minutes, and I'm already tired of holding this here iron. I'd just as soon discharge it and lighten it some."

"That's not very friendly."

"Now you got one minute."

"I'm Custis Long, deputy U.S. marshal. I'd like to ask Sim about that prisoner he identified as Flem Cutter."

"Why?"

"Cutter was killed yesterday when his gang blew up the jail trying to break him out. Sheriff Dan Tompkins was killed in the same blast."

"I know all about that, Deputy," she told him, a look of grim satisfaction on her face. "What happened to that fool sheriff is no skin off my nose."

Patiently, Longarm pressed on. "Is Sim Bond around?"

"He's on his horse, Deputy, ramrodding our crew—doing what he gets paid to do. You think I pay my hands to hang around the ranch all day, getting fat on doughnuts?"

"If you could tell me where you sent the crew today, maybe I could overtake him."

"You won't do nothin' of the sort, Marshal. That man's working for the Jinglebob. Not for you." Abruptly, she aimed the shotgun's yawning twin bores at Longarm. "Your minute's up. Get back on that horse and count your lucky stars, mister. You're the bastard killed my boy. He wasn't worth a bucket of warm spit, but he was my son. Next

38

time I meet you with a Greener in my hand, I'll blow you in two." She smiled; her teeth were short and yellow. "It don't matter what happens to me. I've lived too long as it is. Now git, before I change my mind."

Longarm ascended the veranda steps, and before the old woman could guess what he was about, snatched the shotgun out of her crippled hands. He broke open the weapon, dumped its loads out onto the ground in front of the veranda, then closed the weapon and handed it back to her.

Descending the stairs, he said, "That's so you don't take it in your mind to shoot me in the back."

He mounted up, pulled his horse around, and rode out.

The three men riding into Pine Hill were not members of Brian Levinson's Jinglebob crew. The names they went by were Dutch Dorfman, Gimpy Winslow, and Studs O'Hanlon. Dorfman, riding a feisty black saddle horse he'd stolen from the U.S. cavalry in Oklahoma, was the leader. A hawk-faced killer, he was a bit of a dude, sporting a white Stetson, black frock coat and pants, and sixty-dollar black boots.

Gimpy Winslow rode a fat mare. He was a fierce, bent wreck of a man, as mean as perpetual pain can make a man, with a patch over one gouged-out eye. His yellow teeth were like fangs and he liked his job—whenever it gave him an opportunity to take out his meanness on others, that is, especially when they were unarmed and helpless.

39

Women he liked to beat on mostly, though kids and cripples like himself would serve nicely in a pinch.

Studs O'Hanlon rode a handsome chestnut he'd taken from in front of a saloon in Waco late one night. He was a blond, rosy-cheeked young man of nineteen from Chicago who had come west to emulate the killers in the Ned Buntline books he had been devouring. It was his contention that the rustlers and highwaymen invariably apprehended or shot down by Fearless Ned or Buffalo Bill in those tales hadn't been as smart as he was. He kept his pearl-handled sixgun immaculate, practiced his quick draw tirelessly, and had cold blue eyes—a young devil come early to his kingdom.

Brian Levinson had recruited these three gunslicks in Texas, hoping to make use of their special abilities, talents designed specifically for rousting stubborn settlers, driving off the stock of cattlemen Levinson wanted out of his way, and—just recently—blowing up a jailhouse.

Now, secure in the knowledge that their powerful paymaster would soon be the county sheriff, the three men crossed the train tracks and rode boldly down the broad main drag, turning finally into the hitch rail in front of The Drover's Home. Dismounting, the three men strode into the saloon. Except for the swamper, the only one in the place was Bull Danham. He was behind the bar, busy restocking his shelves. That morning in their line shack, Levinson had described to them what part Bull had played in Slope's death, and each one of the men knew that the saloon's part owner was the son of a bitch who'd gone after Slope with a sawed-off pool cue.

As the three men strode toward the bar, the flapping batwings caused Bull Dunham to straighten up and glance in their direction.

"It's too early gents," he said. "We're closed till noon."

Grinning, Dutch continued on to the bar. "Had a little excitement in here yesterday, huh?"

"That's right."

"I hear you got Slope's blood all over your nice mahogany bar."

Gimpy and Studs were smiling too as they leaned on the bar and sized up Bull. The barkeep was no stranger to trouble, and he sensed that these three meant trouble—in payment, he guessed, for what had happened in the place the day before.

"What're you three after?" he demanded.

"You roughed up a friend of ours," said Studs.

"A dear friend," repeated Gimpy.

"And then you let some bastard gut-shoot him," Dutch said. He turned to look at each of his partners in turn. "Ain't that the way it was, boys?"

"Yep," said Gimpy.

"That's what we heard, all right," said Studs.

"You heard wrong then," said Bull. "Slope came in here drunk and tried to rough up Meg."

"Meg?" repeated Dutch. "Ain't she the whore you call your wife?"

"Hey! Where do you get—"

Bull shut up quickly when he saw the drawn gun in Studs's hand. Then Gimpy pulled a pool cue from his right boot, and reaching over the bar, slammed Bull on the forehead. As Bull cried out and hung groggily onto the edge of the bar, Studs leaped over the bar, took the cue from Gimpy, and proceeded to thrash Bull brutally until Bull sagged unconscious to the floor.

Studs tossed the cue back to Gimpy, jumped back over the bar, and followed Dutch and Gimpy as they headed for the stairs leading to Meg's upstairs apartment. They paid no attention to the swamper, who had dropped his mop and was now running for the back alley door.

Meg, having slept late, had just finished her housekeeping chores and was sitting down in the living room to finish her cup of coffee when the sharp knock came on her door. Not knowing where Longarm had gone or when he might return, she hurried to answer the door, hoping it would be him.

Instead, three men were standing on the landing. One look at two of the men's disreputable, unkempt appearance—not to mention their powerful, horsey smell—and she attempted to slam the door in their faces.

"Not so fast, whore," said the tallest of the three, a hawk-nosed dandy. Dressed all in black, he had on a white Stetson.

He pushed the door back easily with one hand and marched into the apartment, his two disheveled partners following him. One was an old man, the other a kid, the three radiating a mean, vengeful air as they backed her into her apartment, glancing about them as they did. Apparently they were looking to see who else might be in the apartment with her.

Halting with sudden, stubborn resolve in the middle of the living room, Meg said, "What are you men doing in here?"

"Just lookin' around, Meg," said the dandy.

"Get out of here! You have no right in here."

The hawk-faced one reached out, grabbed the front of her house-coat, and pulled her close. "We got the right, bitch," he told her, his face close, "because there's three of us!"

He flung her down onto the couch.

"Search the place," he told his partners. "See if the bastard's still up here."

Meg was frightened now. "Who . . . who're you looking for?"

"Your lover," snapped the dandy. "The deputy marshal you took up here last night, the bastard who killed Slope."

Passing her, the kid bent over her grinning and almost casually ripped her pink housecoat down the front. This early she was not wearing a chemise and she had not put on her corset. With a startled cry, she snatched at the remnants of her housecoat and held them up before her exposed breasts.

"My, my," said the old one, his gimlet eyes gleaming. "Ain't that lovely white meat we got there."

43

He continued past her to search the kitchen, while the kid looked into the bedroom. They both came back into the living room, shaking their heads at their leader.

"He's lit out, Dutch," said the kid.

Dutch looked down at Meg. "Where'd he go, bitch?"

"I don't know."

"Bullshit. You know, you just won't tell us."

"That's not true. If I knew, I'd tell you."

"That so? That ain't being very loyal to your man."

"I'm not worrying. Custis Long won't have any trouble dealing with you three cockroaches."

Dutch slapped her, hard. Then, after waiting for her to look back up at him, he slapped her again.

"Let's have a little more respect," he said. "Now where's that bastard gone?"

"I told you I don't know," she cried, holding her palm up to her flaming cheek.

Dutch turned to the kid. "Okay, Studs, you go first. Take her into the bedroom."

Grinning with anticipation, Studs grabbed Meg and slung her over his right shoulder. All the way into the bedroom, Meg kicked furiously and pounded Studs on the back with her small, ineffectual fists. Studs was still laughing when he flung her down onto the bed and finished ripping off what remained of her housecoat.

As he dropped his gunbelt and peeled down his britches, she started to scream. He slapped her repeatedly until she was too dazed to scream any more, then he dropped onto her, his unclean stench almost overpowering her. She was sobbing helplessly now, no longer able to fight, capable only of enduring this attack.

After the kid had expended himself, the old man came next. Wheezing eagerly, his breath foul, he clambered aboard Meg, but soon found that his ability was severely impaired by his age. Whining with anxiety, he demanded she French him to help him along. When she refused, his maniacal fury was such that when Dutch finally pulled him off her, Meg was in shock.

Bending over her, Dutch said, "I ain't had my helpin' yet, bitch. But I'm rarin' to go. You goin' to tell me where that deputy is?"

Unable to respond, she just looked at him.

"All right, just tell me when he's comin' back."

Again, she could not manage a reply. All of a sudden she began to cry, the sobs bursting explosively out of her.

"Stop crying, damn you," Dutch replied as he dropped onto her, shoving her thighs roughly apart. "Stop crying."

But she could not.

Unable to enter her, Dutch began to slap her in hopes of quieting her down. She made an effort to control her sobbing, but it was impossible. She'd held back until now, but could hold off no longer. When Dutch's slapping continued, and then the punching began, she drifted off into merciful oblivion, still sobbing uncontrollably.

• • •

As Longarm rode back in, the crowd beginning to gather in front of The Drover's Home alerted him. He lifted his mount to an easy lope and swung down hurriedly in front of the saloon. The crowd parted for him as he mounted the porch and pushed through the saloon's batwings.

Bull Dunham was slumped in a chair close to the bar, his head a bloody mess, a doctor working over him. The sawbones didn't impress Longarm much. Still wearing the derby hat that covered his head, he had an enormous potbelly, his pants were greasy, his white cotton shirt was filthy; and as Longarm got closer, he caught the cheap whiskey stench that hung over the physician like a curse.

"What happened?" Longarm asked him.

"Three men rode in a half hour ago," said the doc, glancing up momentarily from his patient. He was dabbing at Bull's broken, bleeding visage with a bloody cotton swab dipped in whiskey. Every time he touched Bull's face with it, the barkeep jerked convulsively. "They used a sawed-off cue stick on him, looks like."

"Where the hell were them two deputies?"

"Soon as the three riders rode in, them two rode out."

"You sure of that Doc?"

"I'm sure of it. Seems like they got a streak of mustard down their backs. We're sure goin' to miss Dan Tompkins, I'm thinking."

Bull spoke up then. "That you, Marshall?"

46

Bull's voice, sounding hollow and cracked, came from a blood-caked hole where his mouth should have been.

"Yeah, it's me."

"Go up and get 'em for me, will ya? They're still in Meg's apartment."

"Jesus, why didn't you say so sooner?"

Longarm ducked around Bull and the doc, and drawing his .44, burst through the door opening onto the stairwell. Halfway up the stairs to the third-floor landing, a sharp-faced hombre in a white hat peered over the railing, then sent a slug crashing through a balustrade behind Longarm. He flattened himself against the wall.

He heard the footsteps of two others joining the first on the landing. Hushed, hurried whispers were followed by the sound of a window sash being flung up. Furious at the thought of them getting away, Longarm charged on up the stairs, his double-action thundering in his hand, some rounds ricocheting off the bannisters, shattered wall plaster filling the air with a fine dust. Reaching the second-floor hallway, he caught sight of an open window and a blond kid dropping from sight.

Reaching the open window, Longarm peered down. A fusillade of gunfire came at him from the shed roof below the window. He ducked back as the windowpanes over his head shattered, showering him with shards of glass. When he looked again, the three men had dropped off the shed roof and were racing down the alley, heading for the main drag. When they vanished from his line of vision, he heard the outcries of furious citizens as the three burst among them. A moment later Longarm saw them on horseback, galloping into sight beyond the hotel. He made careful note of each rider, the horseflesh they were riding especially, then noted the direction they took as they put the town behind them.

He pulled his head in and hurried down the hall to check on Meg. Knocking sharply on the door, he pushed it open, saw nothing out of order in the living room, then heard Meg's faint cry from the bedroom. He entered it, took one look at her sprawled, naked figure, swore angrily, then ducked into a closet. Yanking a red housecoat off a hangar, he flung it over her. She grabbed it gratefully and pulled it up to her neck.

"You don't look so hot," he told her softly, bending over her face.

"Them bastards, Custis," she whispered fiercely. "They took it from me."

He sat down carefully on the bed beside her, the sight of her filling him with a terrible cold rage. He reached over and placed his right hand gently against her swollen cheek. There was a purplish mouse under one eye, which was rapidly swelling shut; her nose was grotesquely distended as one nostril was caked shut with the blood that had filled it earlier; and so swollen was her lower lip that it looked almost as if she were pouting.

"They wanted me to tell where you'd gone," she told him.

"Then it's me they're after?"

"And me too—for Slope's killing."

"That means Brian Levinson sent them."

She nodded.

"You ever see any of them before this?"

She shook her head.

"But here they are, coming out of the woodwork, not caring what they do or who sees them. Looks like they're pretty damn sure Levinson's going to be the next sheriff."

"He is, Custis," she told him through slitted lips. "No one will dare go against him. You got to get out of here before they kill you."

"No," he said, shaking his head decisively. "I'm not going anywhere. Not yet, anyway."

"Custis, listen. He's the head of the county council. He owns half of the town, including the bank. And his Jinglebob is getting bigger every day. You can't stop him. No one can. He's too powerful."

"And his ma's no pushover either."

A faint smile lit her battered features. "You met her then."

"I met her—and her shotgun. Stay quiet now. I'll go down and get the doc. He was working on your husband when I got here."

"Bull? How bad is he?"

"Bad enough. The doc said they used a pool cue on him."

"That poor man. He's had nothing but trouble since he threw in with me. And now you're involved. I'm sorry, Custis."

"Hey, none of that talk, you hear? Now let me go get the doc."

She reached up and grabbed his coat sleeve. "No, Custis. Please. I don't want that smelly old drunk poking at me."

"I just can't leave you here like this."

"Tell the swamper to get Marie, my housekeeper. She lives only a few blocks away. She'll help me bathe and get cleaned up."

Longarm got up from the bed and looked down at her. "All right, then. If that's what you want."

"Thanks, Custis—now, get the hell out of here. I can't stand the thought of you looking at me with my face such a mess. Please."

Encouraged by her sudden concern for her appearance, Longarm bent and kissed her swollen lips. "You'll be as good as new before long, Meg."

As he strode from the room, she called softly "Custis?"

He looked back at her. "Yeah?"

"Be careful."

"Count on it," he said, and left.

Chapter 4

Longarm read the telegram once more before he gave it to the telegrapher.

WILLIAM VAIL
UNITED STATES MARSHAL
FIRST DISTRICT COURT
DENVER, COLORADO

CUTTER BLOWN UP IN ESCAPE ATTEMPT STOP
SHERIFF DAN TOMPKINS ALSO DEAD IN BLAST
STOP BOTH DEATHS SUSPICIOUS STOP STAYING
HERE TO INVESTIGATE STOP DON'T WAIT UP
FOR ME STOP

US DEPUTY MARSHAL, CUSTIS LONG

Longarm handed the message to the old man, who squinted at it through his steel-rimmed glasses, his lips moving silently as he read, then counted the words in order to compute the price of the telegram. Longarm paid him and left the train station. As sure as bears shit in the woods, Longarm realized, the telegrapher would be letting on to his friends about town that the U.S. marshal who'd just arrived to pick up that outlaw was staying on now to do some investigating.

He crossed the street, passed the hotel, and kept going to the sheriff's office. Mounting the low porch steps, he pushed through the door and found the two deputies had returned to town—now that the coast was clear. Seth was reclining on an army cot along one wall; Cal sat behind the sheriff's desk. As Longarm came to a halt in front of the desk, Seth swung his feet off the cot. Cal leaned back in the swivel chair and chucked his hat off his forehead.

"You about ready to pull out, Marshall?"

"Not exactly."

Cal frowned. "That outlaw we brought in's asleep in a pine box—and right alongside of him is the sheriff. What reason you got to hang around?"

From the cot, Seth said, "It ain't healthy for you in this town, not anymore, Marshal."

"You warning me, are you?"

"Hell, no. I'm just telling you like it is, that's all."

"That why you turds ran for cover when them three gunslicks rode in this morning?"

"Hey, now," said Cal, tilting his swivel chair closer. "You got no call to speak to us like that."

"Besides," said Seth, "all we did was just figure what side our bread was buttered on."

"So now you two are dancing to Brian Levinson's tune."

"You can put it that way if you want," said Cal. "He'll be sheriff soon enough. So why argue with the man?"

"Because he's the one responsible for Dan Tompkins's death."

Cal was amazed. "He's what?"

"You heard me."

"You must be plumb loco. That was an accident! Everyone knows that."

"I can prove what I just said," Longarm told Cal.

Seth spoke up then. "Don't pay no attention to him, Cal."

Cal ignored Seth. "All right, mister, prove it."

"What were you two doing when them riders tried to free the prisoner?"

"We was down the street. Seth here was in trouble," Cal said. "He got tangled up with Slope. So I went to help him."

"Only you found he wasn't drunk, that it wasn't as serious as you thought."

"Yeah. Something like that."

"And while you two were dealing with Slope, the jail gets blown up and the sheriff is killed."

"What are you saying? That it was *planned* that way?"

"That's just what I am saying, and my bet is

that your buddy Seth knows all about it."

Cal swiveled his head to glare at Seth. "Jesus, Seth! This man tellin' the truth?"

"He's just beating his gums, Cal," Seth said. "We don't have no reason for believin' anything he says."

"Yeah, Marshal," Cal said. "What proof you got?"

"First off, that prisoner Seth brought in was not Flem Cutter. He was a ringer. He was put in that jail to play his part in the sheriff's murder."

"That's just plain crazy," insisted Seth.

"Not so crazy," Longarm told him. "That description you gave me was not one that matched Flem Cutter's. Whoever you locked into that cell was not the man I came up here to bring back to Denver."

"But that don't make no sense," Cal protested.

"Sure it does. No one was trying to spring Cutter. The object was to blow up the sheriff—and make it look like it was a botched attempt to free Cutter."

"But why?"

"You that blind, Seth? How else was Brian Levinson going to become the next sheriff? This town was solidly behind Sheriff Dan Tompkins. With Tompkins alive, Levinson didn't have a chance."

"Goddammit, Seth," Cal demanded, turning on his partner. "Is that right? Did you know that prisoner was not Flem Cutter?"

"You goin' to believe this guy, Cal?" Seth blustered. "Besides, what difference does it make now?"

With a bitter curse, Cal turned back to Long-arm. "Honest to God, Marshal. I had no idea what was going on."

"Maybe not, but you went along with Seth this morning—even though you knew why those three riders were coming into town."

"That was different. You can't expect Brian Levinson to let you get away with killing his brother."

"Half brother."

"That don't make no difference."

"And I suppose it makes no difference that Slope was shot down in self-defense with a saloon full of witnesses—or that those three men raped Meg and beat up Bull Danham so bad the doc says there's a chance he might not pull through."

Cal slumped forward on his elbows and stared past Longarm out the door. "Oh, shit," he said. "What a goddamn stinkin' mess."

Seth moistened dry lips. "What . . . what d'you want us to do?"

"Get out of here, take the next train out."

"Leave town?"

"The sooner the better. That's why I stopped in here. I figure having two Judases at my back could be a mite dangerous in the days ahead."

"And if we don't?" Seth asked.

"I'll keep both of you in chains until the jail gets rebuilt. Then I'll lock you up until I can take you back to Denver to stand trial for complicity in the murder of Dan Tompkins. It won't take no time at all for me to get the warrants."

"You'll never make it stick."

But Cal knew better. He unpinned his star, dropped it onto the desk, and strode out of the office.

Watching him go, Seth hesitated.

"What'll it be, Seth?" Longarm prodded.

"Aw, shit. I never did like this job."

Seth flung his star at Longarm's feet and hurried out after Cal.

Brian Levinson put his mount down into the ravine that crowded the stream, then followed it out of the ravine, emerging onto a gently rolling, grass-covered flat. At its far end, on a slight rise that gave a spectacular view of the valley and the mountain peaks beyond, sat the Circle T's modest two-story frame house, its bunkhouse, sheds, and corrals surrounding it.

As Brian rode across the flat, he caught sight of Ruthanne Tremaine lugging two wooden buckets of water toward the ranch house, her long apron and wide skirts billowing, her flaxen hair unruly in the wind. As he got closer, the steady thump of his horse's hooves on the flat's solid grass floor caused her to set down the buckets and look in his direction. He saw her shade her eyes as she watched him approach. He couldn't be certain, but it appeared that she stiffened slightly.

He waved.

She waved back, but without the enthusiasm he had hoped to see. She picked up the buckets and continued on to the house, disappearing behind it on her way into the kitchen. He smiled somewhat bleakly and told himself that he wasn't all that bothered by her tepid wave, that before long she would see things his way. Stubborn she was, and hard to please, and maybe a mite proud, but one thing was for certain. She was a realist and knew what side her bread was buttered on. Struggling to make this ranch go was taking its toll, and there were times when she almost found herself unable to make her payroll. What she needed was a man to throw in with her, someone with money and power.

His horse splashed across the shallow stream and gained the far side, kept on, and dug its way up onto the knoll. He nudged it to his left and kept on through the whitewashed corral gate. The Mex cook was standing in the cookshack doorway, and a moment later the beat-up cowpoke Ruthanne kept on as horse wrangler emerged from the barn, a hay fork in his hand. The rest of her crew was not about. Brian assumed they were off riding fence or somewhere in the canyons looking for strays. The fall roundup was getting near.

Neither cook nor wrangler waved at Brian or acknowledged his presence in any way beyond their cold, unfriendly stares. Ignoring them both, Brian rode on toward the big house. Ruthanne pushed through the front door and stepped out onto the veranda. She had tied her hair back and removed her apron. He reined to a halt in front of the hitch rack.

"Mornin', Ruthanne," he said, touching his hat brim in salute.

"Good morning, Brian," she said. "Lemonade?"

Brian swung off his horse. "If it's cold enough."

She disappeared back into the house. Brian ascended the steps and slumped into the wide, comfortable wicker chair sitting on the veranda beside the table. Leaning back, he looked on down the valley, pleased as ever with the view, anxious to make it part of his life one of these days.

Easy, boy, he cautioned. No sense in getting ahead of yourself. All good things take time.

Ruthanne came out carrying a tray with a pitcher of lemonade and two glasses sitting on it. She put the tray down on the table between the chairs, filled his glass, then her own, and sat down.

"I was ready for this rest," she told him. "Been washing since breakfast."

He took a gulp of the lemonade, wishing mildly that he could sweeten it with something a little stronger. "Still lugging the water in from that well, I see," he commented. "Ain't it about time you got the pump brought inside? Wouldn't take all that much to pipe it in."

"I don't mind." She sipped the lemonade and leaned back in her chair, sighing deeply.

As always, he could not keep his eyes off her. She was maybe not beautiful, but the strength in her face had always attracted him. Her eyes were a wonderful lake blue, her high cheekbones prominent, her mouth a proud, assertive line.

58

"It's just that you needn't have to labor like that," he told her.

"I know," Ruthanne said wearily. "You could make it all very easy for me, couldn't you, Brian." She laughed softly. "My God, don't you ever give up?"

"I wouldn't be where I was now if I did."

She looked at him sharply. "Brian, where *are* you now? Do you know?"

"Of course I do."

"No, I don't think you do. And that's why I'll never bend to your will."

"You make it sound pretty ominous."

"It is ominous, Brian. You're trying to buy out or drive out every settler and cattleman in this valley. Why? You have wealth, a fine spread. Why must you have more?"

He thought of telling her then of the sheriff's death, which meant he would now be unopposed in the upcoming election, but a warning voice deep inside him told him to say nothing. Let her find out from someone else, when things had cooled down a bit, the next time she went into town. And that could be a while, he realized, since she took her flatbed into town for shopping only once a month, and her ranch hands—a notoriously protective bunch—spent little time in town, preferring to remain out here with her.

"It's not that I want more," he explained lamely. "It's just that I've got plans."

"*Your* plans? Or is it the Grand Northern's plans?"

"Ruthanne, that spur line will bring unprecedented prosperity."

She sighed and shook her head. "For you, maybe. But for too many others it will be a disaster."

He shrugged. The two of them had been all through this many times, and he was long since weary of the debate. Those settlers and cattlemen she worried so much about had no appetite for losing all that land to provide a right of way for the spur line, and Brian understood perfectly their anger at the prospect. But it was no skin off his nose. It was not his range that was being carved up; and after this spur got built, there'd be no threat to his land for as long ahead as he cared to look. Meanwhile, Pine Hill would boom, his saloon and general store along with it; and for his part in the deal, he'd be tucking away sizable shares in the Grand Northern. He'd be sitting pretty, and all he wanted now was for Ruthanne Tremaine to be sitting there beside him.

"What're you doing this far out, Brian?"

"I'm on my way out to the North Canyon line shack."

"You must've started early."

"I did that."

"Who are those men, Brian?"

He frowned, wondering how much she knew of the bunch he had hired, and disturbed that she knew anything at all about them.

"What men?"

"One of my riders chased a bunch of yearlings almost to North Canyon a few days ago. The three

60

riders who confronted him were not polite. In fact, they threatened him, told him to keep off your land."

"I'll talk to them. No need for them to threaten any of your hands."

"Who *are* they?"

"Jinglebob hands, that's all."

"From the description I got, Brian, they didn't appear to working cowhands. Hired gunslicks is what they looked like."

"You mean that's what your rider thought."

"No, that's what I thought when he described them to me."

Irritated, he shrugged. "Forget it, Ruthanne. Those men are working for me. Maybe they're a little too enthusiastic. Forget about it. I'll talk to them. They won't be bothering you none."

"Maybe not me—but what about Eben Heath?"

He shifted uncomfortably, and to gain time filled his glass with more lemonade. "That sodbuster's got no right here. This is cattle country."

"He's been a good neighbor to me, and he's never refused water to any cattleman."

"That don't make any difference. They plow up the ground, ruin good grazing—and breed like lice."

He glanced at Ruthanne and saw the grim set to her jaw, the cold icy look in her blue eyes, and knew he had blundered. Damn! It was so goddamn hard to keep himself in line around her. She was like his mother. Unforgiving. He caught himself, and mentally composed a short speech that might take the curse off what he had just said.

"Listen, I know I just spoke out of turn. For that I'm sorry. But the Grand Northern's offered Eben three times what his land's worth, and he won't even consider it."

"Why should he? It's his homestead. He's proved it out, and he's got a lovely spot. I certainly wouldn't move out if I were him."

"But Ruthanne, he's smack on the right of way. If he don't cooperate, the spur will have to circle his entire south flat."

"Now isn't that just too bad."

He wanted to slap her, but he bit his lip and said nothing. She was sitting up stiffly in her chair now, staring out over the valley, obviously waiting for him to finish the lemonade and leave. She was too polite to tell him to get on his horse, but he could tell this was how she felt, and he cursed himself for having made this detour. He had done it on impulse, and it had been a mistake.

He slapped his empty glass down on the tray and stood up. Ruthanne got to her feet also.

"Nice of you to stop by, Brian," she told him.

"Yeah. Well, maybe in a little while you and I can get together again. The Cattlemen's Dance is a couple of weeks away. You mind if I take you?"

"Of course not, Brian—if that's what you want."

"You know what I want, Ruthanne."

She did not reply to that.

He left the veranda, slipped the reins off the hitch rack, and swung aboard his mount. He leaned back in the saddle and touched his hat brim to her. "Much obliged for the lemonade, Ruthanne. It really hit the spot."

"Thanks for the visit, Brian. Come again."

He pulled his horse around and rode out. Beyond the gate in the corral, he glanced back to wave good-bye, but Ruthanne was no longer on the veranda. She had gone back inside.

To finish her wash.

Conscious of his defeat, unable any longer to deny what was so obvious—that Ruthanne had no place in her heart for him—Brian came to a sudden decision. No longer would he apologize to Ruthanne for doing what he had to do. And to show her he was his own man, he'd hold back no longer. Even as he came to this decision, he shaded his horse to the north toward the canyon line shack. As soon as those three got back from Pine Hill, he'd hold off no longer. He'd send them against that sodbuster. Burn the bastard out.

It didn't matter now what Ruthanne thought of him. Hell, there were plenty of other fish in the sea. But he could not fool himself. Despite his resolve to ignore her, it did nothing to cure the hollow, angry sense of loss he felt.

The conductor called, "All aboard!"

The train began to move.

"All right, gents," Longarm said. "Get on."

Seth hung back for a minute, looking beyond Longarm as if he expected someone on a white horse to gallop into view and save him from this ignominious fate; but Cal picked up his carpetbag without a murmur and swung aboard the moving train. Seeing this, Seth dumped his own luggage—a battered leather suitcase with one strap missing—up onto the top step, then swung aboard after it.

Longarm stepped back. The train's flanged wheels grumbled more swiftly over the steel rails. Tiny bits of soot flew in his face. He glanced away, and when he looked back Seth and Cal had moved on into the coach. He saw them settle into a seat. In a moment the train had swept out of the station, carrying the two ex-deputies with it.

That done, Longarm left the station, walked down the street to The Drover's Home saloon, and entered. It was late in the afternoon. Ordinarily at this hour the place would be packed. But not today. It was as empty as a church on Monday morning. Longarm walked the length of the bar and pushed into Bull's quarters, a small two-room apartment. Bull was resting on his cot, Meg sitting in a wooden chair beside him. Bull's head was swathed in bandages and he was moving restlessly, waving his arms, muttering all the while in a confused, incomprehensible gibberish.

"He doesn't seem any better," Longarm remarked.

Meg nodded in dismal agreement. "He's worse."

"Where's the doc?"

"He just left."

"What'd he say?"

"He said Bull would be lucky to make it through the night."

Longarm nodded. The doc had already confirmed that the men wielding that pool cue had fractured Bull's skull. As a young man back in West-by-God Virginia, Longarm had known of a man kicked in the head by a draft horse. The fellow had lingered for days in much the same condition as Bull was experiencing now.

Longarm plucked up a chair resting against a wall and set it down on the other side of the cot. Sitting astride it, he crossed his arms on the chair's back and looked at Meg.

"This town doesn't have a town constable. That right, Meg?"

"We figured with the county sheriff and two deputies in town, we didn't need any."

"Well, you do now. Your sheriff's been killed and the two deputies have just left town—on my invitation."

"Then we've got no law in town?"

"You didn't have much with them two, Meg. When those three apes rode in this morning, Seth and Cal rode out."

"I know. The bastards."

"Does this town have a governing council or a mayor?"

"Just a town council."

"Who's on it?"

"Bull here. Winthrop, the owner of the barbershop. And a few store owners and merchants."

"What about Brian Levinson?"

"He runs it. He's the council president. Don't forget, Custis. He's a real power in this town. He owns the Cattleman's Rest and the biggest general store in the valley, Levinson's Pine Hill Emporium."

"And he has shares in the local savings bank, I assume."

"More than shares, Custis. He's its president."

"Well, on the town council, he has only one vote."

"Maybe so, but it'll be a cold day in hell when any man in this town votes against him."

"Maybe I can put some steel in their spine—at least until the election of a new sheriff."

She frowned. "What are you up to, Custis?"

"I want the council to appoint me the town marshal."

"They wouldn't dare. Levinson won't let them."

"We'll see when the time comes. Do what you can to convene the town council. How long do you think that might take?"

"A couple of days, maybe more. I'll have to nudge a good friend of mine, Bill Grant, the owner of the feed mill." She smiled fleetingly. "For past favors granted, I'll now ask one in return. He's the council secretary, and if anyone can convene it, he can. But no matter what, Custis, you're going to have to confront Brian Levinson."

"I'm looking forward to it."

"I'll go see Bill Grant as soon as I can."

"Good."

Longarm got up from the chair and placed it

back against the wall. He leaned over and kissed Meg lightly on her bruised cheek, and left.

It was dusk, and Longarm's rented mount was beginning to protest its usage when Longarm saw the lights of a ranch glowing in the distance. He kept on through a shallow stream, and was riding through a gate in the corral when he saw the dark knot of the rancher's crew emerging from the shadows, each one of them armed and wary.

The ranch house's door opened and a woman stood in the block of light. She was carrying a shotgun. He had never seen so many shotgun-toting women in his life.

Longarm reined in. "Just passing by, ma'am," he called. "I'd like to light and water my horse, if it's all right with you."

"What's your name, mister?"

"Long. Custis Long. I'm a U.S. deputy marshal."

"You're a federal marshal?"

Longarm nodded.

"What are you doing out here?"

"I told you. Just riding through."

"Speak plain, mister, or my men'll take your horse and put you afoot."

"If you'll let me get closer, I'll show you my badge and my other identification."

"You ain't told me yet what you're doing out here," she reminded him coldly.

"Investigating a murder."

"Whose murder?"

"The murder of Sheriff Dan Tompkins."

"Dan? Dan's dead?" Her voice revealed graphically the shock she felt.

"Yes, ma'am. Now, if you'll let me ease down off this horse, I'll be glad to explain."

She lowered the shotgun. "Light and rest awhile, Marshal," she told him. "You're welcome to come inside."

As Longarm dismounted, she called out to her wrangler, instructing him to take care of Longarm's mount.

A half hour later Longarm was sitting at the kitchen table, his second mug of steaming coffee before him, his stomach comfortably distended with steak, mashed potatoes smothered in gravy, and a huge wedge of fresh-cooked apple pie. He had just finished telling Ruthanne Tremaine his adventures since arriving the day before in Pine Hill.

Reflecting on what he had told her, Ruthanne said nothing for a moment, then got up for the coffee pot sitting on the stove.

"Slope's death is no loss, Custis," she said, sitting back down and pouring herself a cup of coffee. "But of course, Brian cannot allow his half brother's death to go unpunished. For one thing, his mother would not allow that."

"I know. I met her."

"Oh?"

Longarm related his encounter with her. Ruthanne nodded grimly. "That's Clara, all right. A real harpie. And a very dangerous woman."

"I guessed as much."

"From the way you tell it, Custis, Brian Levinson is responsible, not only for sending those three into Pine Hill after Bull Danham and Meg O'Riley, but also for the death of Dan Tompkins."

"And for corrupting those two deputies."

"It's quite a desperate catalogue. And difficult to believe. But not impossible to believe, I'm afraid."

"You know what Brian Levinson's motive is, of course."

"Yes, he wants to be sheriff," she said bitterly. "Among other things."

"He's a very ambitious man."

"I think it's his mother. She never gives him any credit. He's always trying to impress her, but she's never satisfied. I think you should know, Custis. Brian was here earlier."

"That so?"

"Yes. The interesting thing is, he didn't tell me about his brother's death or the death of Sheriff Tompkins."

"What was he doing here? Isn't this some distance from his spread?"

"Not really. His range land circles mine and reaches well into the foothills north of here. His crewmen often ride through here and I let them water their horses and sit a spell. My lemonade is famous throughout the valley."

"You still haven't told me what he was doing here."

She added more coffee to his mug. "You ready for this, Custis?"

"Shoot."

"Those three men you're after. I think I know where they are."

"Where?"

"Where Brian was heading—in one of Brian's line shacks, the one in North Canyon."

"How far is it from here?"

"It's a good distance, another three hours of hard riding, at least."

"So he's gone out there to pay off them three for services rendered."

"There's something else, Custis. The man who died in that jail cell was a ringer, all right. More than likely, he was the same saddle tramp I fed one night and let sleep in the bunkhouse. When he rode off the next day, he was heading for North Canyon."

"Right into a bear trap."

She nodded.

"That ties it up pretty well. Those three trussed him up and on orders from Brian, Seth brought him in as Flem Cutter. Dan Tompkins had no way of knowing for sure it wasn't Cutter Seth was bringing in. He probably just took Seth's word on it."

"Poor Dan."

"From the sound of things, he was getting to be a mite careless."

"Yes. I'm afraid so."

"Thanks for the feast, Ruthanne. I guess I'll be

moving out now. I'd sure appreciate some directions to get to North Canyon."

"Stay here, Custis. It's too late for you to go now. It'll be close to midnight before you reach that canyon, and what can one man do against Brian and those three gunslicks he's hired?"

"You offering me help?"

"I'm offering more than that, Custis."

He looked across the table and found himself lost in the incredible beauty of her lake-blue eyes. She was a handsome, bold woman, almost as tall as he, and from the moment he followed her into the ranch house, he had found her as attractive as she now obviously found him.

Smiling, he reached out and rested his hand on hers. "I don't want to sound like a wet blanket, but do you think that would be wise?"

"I've been widowed for seven years. You've heard of the seven-year itch? Well, I've got it, Custis. Only I can't go in town and scratch it for a price, the way you men can. And any woman who lets her ramrod sleep with her has pretty damn soon lost all control over her crew and her spread's operation. I've seen it happen to others and I know."

"What about Brian? From what you tell me, he's been very attentive of late."

"He has, yes. And that's the frightening part of it. He's a big man, bluff, with all the assertiveness one likes to see in a man. You have no idea how that appeals to a woman. And may God forgive me, there are times when I do find myself

71

thinking of him in that way. Even today, as he sat beside me on the porch, I could feel myself warming to him."

"Well, then."

"Custis, Brian's a weak, twisted man. What you've told me this past hour has only verified what I've felt for years. He's a man capable of anything. I think I'd rather die than succumb to his blandishments."

He grinned at her. "So it looks like I'm it then."

"Yes," she said, smiling warmly back at him. "You walked into a bear trap too, it seems."

"First off, I'd like a bath. Can that be arranged?"

"Of course," she said, glowing. "Ah, Custis, it will do my sinful heart good to see a naked man once again."

He laughed out loud, then finished his coffee.

Chapter 5

Brian leaned forward in his saddle as his mount struggled up the steep trail. Two ravens perched on a lightning-blasted pine protested his appearance on the slope, then flapped away. Brian reached the crest and saw Gimpy step out from behind a tree, a rifle in his hand.

"Hello, there, Mr. Levinson."

Brian pulled up and dismounted. "Where's the other two?"

"In the shack. You want me to take the horse around back?"

"I'd appreciate it." Brian handed the reins to the old man. "How'd it go this morning?"

"We did some damage."

Brian frowned, not too pleased with that response, but he shook off his displeasure and strode on past Gimpy. The old man sent a shudder up his spine, reminding Brian of a mangy dog, eager to bite the hand that fed it. Keeping ahead of Gimpy, he reached the line shack and pushed into it without knocking. The wood stove was thundering, a pot of steaming water sitting on it. Near the window Dorfman was shaving himself, his mirror propped up on the top bunk. As Brian entered, he turned, his razor gleaming in the sunlight coming through the window.

"Well, well," Dorfman said. "Howdy, Mr. Boss Man."

Studs O'Hanlon, lying on his back on the lower bunk, cocked an eyebrow at Brian. "Hello, Brian."

Brian wasn't sure he liked their response to his arrival, but the long ride out here to the line shack had made him too weary to demand the respect he felt he deserved.

"Yeah, I'm back," he said, his voice grating. "This here's my line shack, remember?"

"Oh, oh. Brian's mad," Studs said, grinning.

Dorfman had turned back to the mirror, and was pulling the skin tight over his jawline as he guided the razor. Speaking carefully, he asked, "You got another job for us, Mr. Boss Man?"

"Don't call me Boss Man," Brian snapped, slumping into a chair. "I don't like it."

He caught the warning glance that passed between Dutch and Studs. Their boss had a hair across his ass, and they'd better be nice. Or at least careful. Studs sat up on the bunk and rested his feet on the dirt floor, his head leaning out to avoid the top bunk's frame.

"First of all," Brian told them, "I want to know how it went this morning."

Dorfman wiped off his face with an old shirt. "Bull Danham's not going to be seeing things very clearly—or talking so good neither. Fact is, we probably turned him into the village idiot."

"We clobbered him with a pool cue," Studs said. "The same thing you said he tried to do to your brother."

"And the U.S. deputy?"

"He wasn't there," Dutch told him.

"You mean you missed him?"

"Not exactly."

"Damn it. Speak plain."

Dutch looked for a long moment at Brian, as if he were losing patience with him, but was willing to give his employer a chance to behave. Brian took a deep breath and sat back on his chair and waited.

"We thought he was still up there in that whore's apartment, so we went up after him. But he was already gone."

"I see," said Brian tightly.

"So what we did was," Dutch continued patiently, "once we knew for certain the U.S. deputy had flown, we took it from the whore—all three of us. We left her feeling pretty bruised and used up, I'd say. Then this crazy deputy marshal charged up the stairs, blazing away at us, so we left by the window and rode out."

"You rode out? The three of you against one man—and you rode out?"

"Now think it over for just a minute, will you?"

"What in the hell is there for me to think over?"

Patiently, Dutch explained. "Beating up on that fool barkeep and raping that saloon gal was one thing. But a U.S. federal marshal is a different kettle of fish, Mr. Boss Man. What we did to that whore got him all stirred up. He saw us light out. I got a feeling he'll be coming after us soon enough."

"And?"

Dutch folded his razor blade into its handle and smiled at Brian. "When he does come after us, we'll be waitin'. We'll blow a hole in him, then slice him up and spread him over the landscape for the buzzards to feed on. He'll just disappear, you see? Then no one will ever know what happened to him, and you won't be combing federal marshals out of your hair."

What Dutch said made good sense, and Brian felt his blood pressure go down some. "All right," he said grudgingly. "We'll let that go and see what happens. The thing is, this plan of yours won't work unless you can make sure that marshal comes out here after you."

"He will, if we can give him more provocation—sort of singe his ass a little."

"Then I think I have just the solution."

"You sending us out again?"

"Tonight. And I'll go with you this time. I want to make sure it gets done right." He didn't like how that sounded, and he could see Dutch and Studs didn't like it either. But they kept their lips buttoned and said nothing. After all, they were in his hire.

"Where we goin', Brian?" Studs asked.

"That nester's place."

"You want us to burn him out?" Studs's eyes gleamed at the prospect, like a kid waiting for the fireworks to begin on the Fourth of July.

"That's what I want."

"I guess we could manage that," Dutch said.

"So let's get moving."

There wasn't much of a moon, but it was giving off enough light for them to get the job done. In fact, it would help keep them well hidden until the fire began. At first he had thought he might want to remain back in the willows flanking the stream and let Dutch and the other two do the job. But their practiced insolence had irritated him so that he'd decided to work right alongside of them, to show that he didn't just give orders and was not afraid to dirty his own hands, if it came to that.

The smell of horses in the rear of the barn was strong, and he could hear them stamping their feet nervously as he entered it. Earlier, the settler's collie had come running toward them from the front of the darkened house, its tail wagging, as ferocious as a butterfly. Gimpy had broken its skull with one swipe of his rifle barrel.

Just behind the three of them, disoriented slightly in the barn's deep gloom, Brian stumbled and cracked his shin against a singletree. He almost went down and, reaching out for something to grab, pulled a tangled clump of harness chains loose from a shelf. The chains struck the wooden floor with a heavy, clanging thump.

Gimpy was just ahead of him. He turned on Brian and snarled, "Why don't you blow a bugle, for Christ sake!"

"Shut up, you two," said Dorfman.

Dorfman had found a lamp and was holding a match to the wick. Once he got it lit, he kept the flame so low it did little more than illuminate his face, which hovered in the darkness like a hellish mask.

"You sure you want to do this, Levinson?" Dorfman asked.

"Yes. We'll push the wagon out of here as soon as we get the fire going. Then set them horses free."

"Why all the concern?"

"I want them to be able to get out of here when this is all over. If the family's afoot, it will cause a real stink. This way, once they drive off with their belongings, in a few weeks nobody will remember."

Dorfman chuckled. "Pretty damn smart, Boss Man," he said. "I got to hand it to you."

Brian was pleased to hear the grudging respect he detected in Dorfman's voice. It was about time.

What happened to Eben once the burning barn drew him from the house had been settled already. There would be no gunfire. Studs would wait for him in the barn, coldcock him with a blow from his revolver, and drag him into the blazing barn so that his charred body would be found the next day, apparently the result of his foolhardy dash into the inferno to save his livestock. As for the settler's cabin, there were no plans for burning it—unless a few blazing cinders or boards happened to be carried onto the cabin's roof by the fierce updraft.

The point was that the burned-out barn would have to be seen as the cause of Eben Heath's death. Brian was not ready for an open confrontation this early in the game, so this had to be as much like an accident as he could make it.

Dorfman increased the light from the lamp and lifted it high so they could continue on through the big doorway leading into the horse stalls. It took no time at all to free the huge draft horses and send them stomping out of the barn into the moonlit pasture. The four men returned to the front of the barn then, and Brian showed he was not too proud to lift the singletree and hold it above the ground as the others pushed the big flatbed wagon out into the yard.

So far, they had made surprisingly little noise, and Brian was pleased at how well things were going. He let down the singletree, and had turned to follow the three men back into the barn, when the settler's back door slammed open and Eben Heath appeared, a shotgun in his hand.

"All right, you bastards," he cried. "Hold it right there!"

Oh, shit, Brian thought.

He whirled and, drawing his sixgun, dropped onto his belly in the tall grass beside the barn's open door. The others scurried deeper into the barn as Eben ran toward it. Watching him come, Brian debated whether he dared shoot. This had not been part of his plan.

Eben Heath settled the matter.

Furious, running full tilt, he discharged one of his barrels at the shadowy figures he detected inside the barn. Brian heard the buckshot whistle over his head and slam into the barn's side. Muttering a curse, he kept his head down as the furious sodbuster continued on toward the barn.

From inside it came a loud pop, the sound of shattered glass, followed by a powerful *whumph* as Dorfman flung the lighted kerosene lamp against a wall. Peering into the barn, Brian saw a red ball of light glowing in the midst of a pall of black smoke as the flames, feeding on the loose hay, raced across the floor and then leaped up the wall. Almost instantly, it seemed, they were feeding on the floor of the loft. Dense, black smoke pumped out through the open barn door.

Groaning aloud in pure despair, Eben pulled up in front of the open barn door, staring in at the barn's flaming interior as the flames grew brighter, and still brighter—sending a garish light over the yard in front of the barn.

Eben caught sight of Brian crouching in the grass.

"Levinson," he cried. "You son of a bitch!"

As he spoke, he flung up his shotgun. But Brian didn't wait for Eben to pull the trigger. He fired, thumb-cocked, and fired again.

With a muffled cry, Eben dropped his shotgun and pitched forward to the ground. Studs ran out of the darkness behind Brian, grabbed the settler under his arms, and hauled him into the barn. A moment later he stumbled out, his right arm over his eyes to protect them from the smoke.

Behind Brian, Dorfman tapped him on the shoulder.

"We better get the hell out of here," he suggested to Brian.

Brian turned. Gimpy was standing beside Dorfman. Beads of dirty sweat were coursing down their faces. By now the heat was so intense, they had no choice but to flee into the trees flanking the barn, after which they paused to look back.

"Well, that's done," Studs said, grinning at Brian.

"Yeah," said Dorfman. "Nice going, Boss Man. You sure took that sodbuster out. I say you did yourself proud."

The trouble was, Brian didn't quite see it that way. As a matter of fact, he felt a little sick. A high, keening scream cut through the night. Brian looked back at the flaming barn and saw Eben's woman rushing across the yard toward the barn. Before any one could even attempt to stop her, she rushed without pause into the barn's flaming maw.

"Oh, shit," muttered Brian.

"We got horses waitin'," Dorfman reminded them, his voice hoarse. "I say it's about time we use them."

"Yeah," said Studs. "She'll never get out of that alive, the damn fool woman."

"Serves her right," muttered Gimpy.

Brian heard a sudden, high-pitched wail as a small boy stumbled out the of the cabin's back door into the night, while from inside came the sobbing cry of an infant. Turning his back on the scene, Brian ran for his horse, the others following after him—as eager as he was to escape the horror of what they had just seen.

Had they not been in such a hurry, a moment or two later they would have seen a remarkable sight: Eben's woman, tiny flames feeding on her long hair and on her nightgown's sleeve, dragging her husband out of the inferno, only a second before the barn's roof crashed with a roar into the leaping flames.

As the early morning sun poured through the bedroom window, Longarm stirred and lifted his head off Ruthanne's bare shoulder.

"Don't move," she said sleepily. "Please. It feels so good with you snug against me."

Reaching over her shoulder, he closed his big palm over her breast and felt her nipple grow hard under his palm.

"It'll feel a whole lot better if you'll roll over."

"Oh?"

She did as he suggested and smiled up at him,

as ready for him as he was for her. He kissed her
on the lips, and was shifting his weight onto her
when shouts from the yard below caused them to
push apart. Snatching her nightgown off the foot
of the bed, Ruthanne slipped into it and tied the
sash, then hurried to the window. Longarm was
out of bed himself by this time; keeping discreetly
behind her, he peered over her shoulder down at
the yard.

A flatbed wagon drawn by two draft horses had
entered the yard. A woman with two children, one
in her arms, the other clutching at her long skirts,
was standing behind the wagon, surrounded by
members of the Circle T crew. As Longarm and
Ruthanne watched, two of the crew jumped down
from the wagon and turned about to help two other
men on the wagon lift down a man's body, after
which they jumped off the tailgate and helped
carry the unconscious man toward the house, the
woman with her two children following.

Ruthanne gasped. "It's Eben Heath," she told
Longarm. "He's been hurt. I must get dressed."

"Go ahead," Longarm said, stepping back out
of her way. "I'll wait a bit and follow you down
afterwards."

"Yes, that would be best," she said.

He sat back down on the bed and watched her
dress, then hurry from the bedroom, her footsteps
swift and light on the stairs. A moment later he
heard her sharp, clear voice directing the men carrying the wounded man into the house.

Longarm pulled on his britches, and despite his

eagerness to get downstairs, forced himself to take his time with his morning toilet, shaving carefully without lather in tepid water. He gave himself a sponge bath, then finished dressing and hurried from the bedroom, took the back stairs to the kitchen, saw Ruthanne busy at the stove, ducked into the sitting room, and a moment later crossed the entrance hall and entered the living room.

The moment he did, he caught the acrid, hospital smell of alcohol and dilute carbolic acid. One look at the wounded man on the sofa, and he knew the settler had sustained serious, perhaps fatal, gunshot wounds. While the Circle T's wrangler tended to his wounds, a man Longarm judged to be the Circle T's ramrod stood behind the wrangler with his arms folded, watching grimly. At the foot of the sofa stood the settler's wife, keeping her two children as calm as she could, though the little boy, a toddler, cried steadily, his big eyes riveted on his father.

Moving closer, Longarm saw that in addition to the bullet wounds high on Eben's chest, there were ugly, puckering burns on his cheekbone and down his side as well. A bullet probe in his gnarled hand, the wrangler was already poking tentatively into one of the chest wounds. Ruthanne hurried out of the kitchen with a pan of steaming water and put it down on the floor beside the sofa. Noting the steaming pan of water's presence with a quick glance, the wrangler went into action. Bending suddenly forward, his head obscuring the two wounds, he plunged the probe in. For an old man he was exceedingly calm as he deftly extracted one slug, dug swiftly into the next wound, and fished out another slug.

Leaning back then, he dropped the bandages he had already folded on the sofa's arm into the pan of hot water, poured dilute carbolic acid into the water and over the bandages, then retrieved the bandages, slapped them down onto Eben's wounds, and began scrubbing them out, doing his best, it seemed, to wake up the still-unconscious settler, goading him to cry out. Once he got the wounds bleeding freely—and cleanly—he moistened fresh bandages in the carbolic-acid-and-water solution and placed them over the entry wounds. Then he got up to give Ruthanne a chance to bandage Eben's chest.

The ramrod handed the wrangler a whiskey flask. The old man took it eagerly and tipped it up, swallowing greedily. "I don't know," the wrangler muttered as he handed the flask back to the ramrod. "He's sure lost a lot of blood, and I don't like the looks of them burns."

"Has anyone sent for the doctor?" Longarm asked.

They all turned to look at him then—as if until that moment no one had been aware of his presence.

"That quack," snorted the wrangler. "What good would he do?"

"He smells some, I admit. But he's been taking pretty good care of Bull Danham."

"What's wrong with Bull?"

85

"He's been beaten badly by a pool cue."

"That same one he uses to dust off trouble-makers?"

"Or one like it."

"Serves him right."

"There's a chance he might die."

"Well, now," the wrangler allowed. "I'm sorry to hear that, but that don't change my opinion about that doc."

Ruthanne had finished tying the bandage around Eben's chest. She sat back on the edge of the sofa and looked down at the unconscious man's still figure, obviously very concerned.

Longarm stepped closer to Ruthanne. "What happened here, anyway?"

Without answering Longarm directly, Ruthanne looked up at Eben's wife. "Yes, Jenny. Who shot Eben? And you mentioned a fire."

"There *was* a fire, Ruthanne," Jenny replied, pulling her boy closer to her as she recalled. "But before that Eben saw some men moving about in the barn, and when he went out after them, someone shot him."

"Who was it?" Longarm asked.

"I didn't see. It was dark, and it all happened so fast. But after the fire started, I saw one of them drag Eben into the barn."

"While it was on fire?"

"Yes."

"My God, how'd he get out?"

"I dragged him out."

"You mean you went in after him?"

"Of course."

It was then that Longarm noted her hair. It was short and discolored in spots, and the sleeve of her nightgown was badly singed, in places partially burnt through. This frail little woman had run into a blazing inferno and dragged her unconscious husband out of it with no thought for her own safety. And as Longarm realized this, so, it seemed, did everyone else in the room as they stared at Jenny in an awed, humble silence.

Ruthanne rushed to her side and put her arms around her, hugging her close. Then she led her and the two children over to an upholstered chair, into which Jenny collapsed. Everyone stared at her, only now realizing how emotionally and physically exhausted she had to be at this moment.

But there were still questions that had to be asked, and Longarm—as patiently as he could manage it—asked one of them. "Jenny, who would do such a thing? Who would shoot your husband and burn down your barn? Who wants to drive you and your husband from this valley?"

Jenny looked up at Longarm, her drawn face set in anger. There was no hesitation as she spat out, "Brian Levinson."

"We need proof, Jenny, so we can nail him," Longarm told her. "You say it was too dark for you to see any of their faces?"

"Yes. But Eben must have seen them. I heard him shouting at one of them before he fired his shotgun."

A groan came from the sofa. Everyone in the room turned to look at Eben. He moved his head slightly, and then his eyes opened and he looked about him in some confusion. Then, focusing his eyes, he caught sight of his wife—and the two children.

"My God, Jenny!" he gasped hoarsely. "What're we doin' here?"

Jenny jumped up from the armchair and flung herself down beside her husband, her children with her. The tears came from her, so grateful was she to see Eben conscious and apparently on the mend.

Longarm stepped closer to the sofa. "Eben, who did this? Who shot you and fired your barn?"

"Levinson," the man gasped. "It was Brian Levinson. He did it!"

With a quiet nod, Longarm left the living room and walked into the kitchen. Ruthanne followed with the foreman and the wrangler, all of them anxious to give Jenny and her husband some privacy.

Ruthanne took this opportunity to introduce Longarm to her foreman, Jim Thompson, and the wrangler, Sam. As the three men seated themselves around the deal table, Ruthanne took a pot of coffee off the stove and filled four coffee mugs.

"Brian's gone wild," she said, joining them at the table.

"He wasn't alone," Longarm said. "He had help. I'll bet on it."

Jim Thompson looked at him. "What kind of help?"

"Three gunslicks who nearly beat Bull Danham to death and raped Meg in town yesterday."

"My God," said Thompson. "They did that?"

"They did, and they're the same bunch, I'll bet, who blew up the jail and killed the sheriff."

"You talkin' about them three gunslicks hiding out in Brian's North Canyon line shack?"

"The same."

"Them bastards," said the wrangler, his eyes blazing with indignation.

Longarm let that news sink in, then looked around the table. "It looks to me like you all want very much to stop Brian Levinson and his gunslicks."

"Of course," said Ruthanne.

"Well, wouldn't it be a lot simpler all around if you had the law on your side?"

"But we don't have the law on our side," Thompson reminded him. "The law's dead. And Levinson killed him, if what you say is true."

"Brian's already sheriff by default," Ruthanne said. "Anyone opposing him now will simply be run out of town."

"Or killed," commented the wrangler.

"And all done nice and legal," Thompson added gloomily.

"Well, now, maybe it doesn't have to be that way," Longarm told them.

"What do you mean?"

"I've already asked Meg O'Riley to convene the

89

town council. When it does convene, I'll demand they elect me town marshal. Once that's done, I'll be able to move on Levinson legally."

"Sure, but what happens in the meantime?" Thompson asked.

"And since when has that council ever gone against Levinson?" Ruthanne pointed out. "He has every council member in his hip pocket."

"I say we stop him now," the wrangler said. "Go up to that line shack and roust them three gunslicks. When they see a hangman's noose, they'll sing like canaries."

"I like that," said Thompson.

"Yes," Ruthanne said quickly, eagerly. "If those three could be made to talk, their testimony— along with Eben's—would make it impossible for the town council to deny Custis's suggestion."

Longarm liked the idea too. He glanced at Thompson. "Do you think you could lead me to that line shack?"

"Sure. You, and the rest of this crew if you want. Hell, once they hear what Eben told us, you won't be able to hold them back."

Longarm turned to Ruthanne. "Stay here with Jenny and Eben. And take good care of Eben. We'll be desperate for his testimony if those gunslicks get away. He's our best witness to what happened last night."

"All right," she said, getting out of her chair to pour them another cup of coffee. "I'll do that—but you men be sure to bring back those three. The more we can get on Brian Levinson, the better it will be for all of us."

"Done," said Longarm.

In less than half an hour, Longarm had unofficially deputized Jim Thompson and the wrangler and was riding out of the Circle T with six good men at his back.

Chapter 6

Brian was a shaken man when he reached the line shack, though he did his best not to let on to the others. He was apparently successful in this, since Dorfman and the other two treated him with a sudden and surprising deference, even respect. They had seen Brian shoot down the sodbuster, had seen him send two rounds into the man's chest, and as far as they were concerned, he had paid his dues and was now a full-fledged member of their club.

It was chilly in the line shack and Gimpy was given the chore of building a fire in the potbelly stove. As Studs got himself comfortable in the lower bunk, Dorfman looked over at Brian, who was standing by the door, watching Gimpy.

"What now, Mr. Levinson?"

"I'm not sure."

"Well, we got a good start on clearing out this valley. Once word gets around what happened down to that nester, it'll take the spine out of them other ranchers you was talkin' about."

"We hope."

"No doubt about it," Dorfman said, grinning. "A charred corpse speaks loud and clear."

"We won't have no trouble now," Studs chimed in, chewing on a piece of hay. "We could use some help, though."

"Maybe some of your crew," Dorfman said.

"I suppose I could manage that," Brian heard himself say.

"They loyal?"

"Of course."

"Well, the more men we have, the sooner we can get this business over with. And the sooner we can pull out with that bonus you mentioned."

"So who do we hit next?" Studs asked from the bunk.

"There's Anchor at the head of the valley, and Sam Winston's Lazy W, closer by."

"Just exactly how do you want us to handle them?" Dorfman asked.

"All we got to do is drive off the rest of their stock," Brian said, somewhat hastily. "My crew's been whittling away at their herds for the past three months."

"Good. That sounds like it won't take long. I'm getting sick of this line shack."

"It ain't no good for my rheumatiz neither," said Gimpy, turning from the stove.

Brian nodded dully in agreement. All this was what he wanted. He had discussed his intentions with Dorfman and his men when he hired them. But what had just happened had shaken his resolve a bit. He had just killed a man, shot him down in cold blood. He was no longer simply making plans. He had stepped over a line. A man's blood was on his hands.

He spied an empty bunk in the far corner and headed for it. As he slumped down onto it, he said to the others, "I'm bushed. We better get some sleep. We can make further plans tomorrow."

"Hey," Gimpy piped up. "Who's gonna keep this stove going? I'm tired too."

"Forget it," said Brian. "We don't need it. It's hot enough in here."

Dorfman grinned at the old man. "You heard what the boss said, Gimpy. Now shut up."

Grumbling, the old man climbed into the bunk above Studs, flopped onto his back, and was asleep in a few minutes, snoring with his mouth open. Studs poked up at the old man until he caused him to flop over onto his stomach and stop snoring.

When Brian woke the next morning, the sleep had done him little good. He was as weary as when he had dropped off. Even the twittering of birds outside the shack depressed him, serving to remind him that he would find it difficult to enjoy again such happy sounds. He pushed himself erect and left the shack to empty his bladder. To his surprise he found the sun was well up over the horizon. They had slept late. For Brian, a man who was always up by dawn, this evidence of his slothfulness seemed only to increase his depression.

To awaken himself fully, he visited the spring behind the shack and vigorously rubbed the icy water over his face and neck. When he returned to the shack, he found that Gimpy had built a fresh fire in the stove and was preparing breakfast. A frying pan filled with salt pork and sliced potatoes sizzled on the stove, a fragrant pot of coffee puffing beside it.

He began to feel a little better.

Dorfman, leaning back against his bunk, was yawning and scratching under his arms. Studs had climbed back into his bunk, his arms folded under his head while he waited for Gimpy to finish preparing breakfast.

"It's late!" Brian told them morosely. "Don't you men ever get off your asses before this?"

"We were up late," Dorfman reminded him with a grin.

"Sure," Studs seconded. "Don't you remember, Mr. Levinson?"

A few moments before, Brian had seen them stumbling into the bright morning, unbuttoning their flies, their voices harsh. They had reminded him of yapping, skulking coyotes. Watching them now in the shack's cramped interior, he realized he wanted now to be rid of their company. Seeing them reminded him of the action he had taken the night before. That they now accepted him so readily as one of their own only made matters worse.

"I'm pulling out," he told them suddenly.

The three men looked at him in surprise.

"Now?" asked Dorfman.

"What's the hurry?" asked Studs, sitting up on the edge of his bunk.

"Didn't you say we was goin' to make more plans?" Dorfman reminded him. "We got them other two ranchers to take care of, don't forget."

"Later. We can make plans later."

"Thing is, you ain't had no breakfast yet," Gimpy reminded him, almost plaintively.

"I ride better on an empty stomach," Brian said.

"You sure are in all-fired hurry to get out of here," Dorfman commented. Brian could see at once the suspicion in his eyes.

"It's late, dammit," Brian told him. "The sun's up already, and . . . I got a brother to bury."

"Oh, yeah," Dorfman said. "I forgot about that."

"Well, looky here," Gimpy said hopefully. "This breakfast is near done. Wouldn't take no time at all for you to gobble it down."

"Gimpy's right, Mr. Levinson," said Studs. "You got a long ride ahead of you. At least hold on for some coffee. That right, Gimpy?"

"Sure," Gimpy cried, reaching for the pot.

"All right," said Brian. "A cup of coffee would go pretty good about now, I guess."

The three seemed mollified, but Brian could tell that Dutch was suspicious of his sudden eagerness to ride out. But Brian didn't care. He drank Gimpy's vile coffee and almost choked on the grits. Spitting them out, he bid the men a hasty good-bye and fled the shack. Dorfman and Studs followed him out, watching him silently as he mounted up.

As Brian swung his horse around, he looked back at them. "You men got enough grub?"

"Yeah," Gimpy said, poking his head out of the shack. "But we's all out of whiskey."

"I'll see to it," Brian told them, clapping spurs to his horse.

As he topped the ridge above the shack a moment later, he looked back at them. Dorfman and Studs were still in front of the line shack. Gimpy as well, shading his eyes as he watched him ride off.

In a very big hurry, and without any breakfast.

About a quarter of an hour later Brian was still on the ridge, his horse picking its way carefully along the rocky spine, when he heard the soft, ominous thunder of charging hoofbeats. He hurriedly reined in his mount, dismounted, and pulled his horse back off the ridge. He returned to the ridge, and from behind a boulder peered down at a trail leading out of a heavy thatch of pine. The first rider broke into the clear, coming on hard, as did the others strung out behind him. The riders were too distant for Brian to make out their faces, but one thing was for sure. This posse was heading for his line shack.

He went back to his horse, pulled a pair of binoculars out of a saddlebag, and focused quickly on the two riders in the lead. One of them was Jim Thompson, the Circle T foreman. But who was this other one riding alongside him? He rode tall in the saddle, was wearing a brown tweed frock coat and snuff-brown Stetson, and had a flaring longhorn mustache. And then Brian realized who this had to be. The deputy U.S. marshal who'd killed Slope.

With a grim chuckle Brian remembered Dorfman telling him why he had not made any great effort to take this deputy marshal in town. He preferred instead to lure him up here so he could leave him for the buzzards. Well, here they come, Dorfman. Good luck. Brian lowered his binoculars and watched the riders sweeping closer, a thin patina of dust hanging in the air over their strung-out formation. He counted eight riders in all.

Brian knew that if he turned back now, he might be able to warn Dorfman and the others in time. For a moment he was certain this was what he should do. But then he considered the matter more closely. These men were the only witness to what had happened last night. Now, all he had to do was let this posse continue on its way. Do nothing and he would be rid of them, free and clear.

Brian left the ridge, stuffed the binoculars back into his saddle-bag, and pulled his mount further off the ridge. Holding his hand over the horse's muzzle to prevent it from greeting the horses passing below, he waited until the steady pound of hoofbeats had faded, then swung into his saddle, clapped spurs to his mount, and headed back to the Jinglebob.

Earlier, watching Levinson ride off, Dutch frowned intently. He didn't like it. Not one bit.

"I think we got trouble," he said aloud.

"Yeah," said Studs. "Our boss man was sure in one big hurry to make tracks."

"Dammit," Gimpy groaned. "I don't think I like this job. How much longer we got to stay out here in this damn shack?"

Without answering Gimpy directly, Studs mused aloud, "Seems like all the man wanted was to get out of here. Like he was runnin' from something."

"I smell a double cross," said Dutch.

"So what do we do?"

"Stay loose. I may be all wet, but we can't take no chances. Gimpy, I want you to climb up onto that ridge and keep an eye out. You see anything, sing out."

"Jesus, Dutch," Gimpy said, shading his eyes as he peered up at the ridge. "You want me to go way the hell up there?"

"Go on, get moving," Dorfman said, pushing the old man so hard Gimpy stumbled and almost went down.

"That ain't fair, Dutch."

"That's right. You're a cripple."

"Let me go too," said Studs. "Hell, this old fart won't do any good up there. He can't see no farther than the end of his nose."

Dorfman shrugged. "All right. Go with him then. Just keep your eyes peeled."

"What are we supposed to be looking for?"

"Trouble."

As the two scrambled up the steep slope, Dorfman saddled his horse and rode out. He followed along the same ridge Levinson had taken, the shack soon out of sight behind him. A half mile or so further on, he saw Levinson, off his horse, peering through a pair of binoculars at a posse charging along the valley below. The posse was heading for the pass through which anyone leaving the valley would have to come.

As he watched, Levinson packed away his binoculars and rode off toward his spread—making no effort at all to return and warn Dutch and the others. This was all the proof Dutch needed as he swung his horse around and, cursing bitterly, headed back to warn the others.

No wonder that bastard had lit out in such a hurry. It didn't have nothin' to do with him getting back in time to bury his brother. He had set them up, which was why, when he found out how late he had slept, he'd been in such an all-fired hurry to escape the shack before the posse got there.

As his mount picked its way off the ridge down to the shack a few minutes later, Dorfman called out to Studs and Gimpy. Standing up on the ledge, they peered down at him.

"What's up?" Studs called.

"Riders coming hard. A posse!"

"We can't see nothin'!"

"Stay up there long enough and you will."

"What'll we do?" asked Studs.

"We're ready for them. Pick 'em off as they come up that slope. I'll stay down here to back your play."

"Here they come!" Gimpy cried, pointing.

Dutch checked the load on his sixgun, then slipped a cartridge into the empty sixth chamber.

Before they reached the pass, Longarm and the posse performed a maneuver they had settled on earlier. While Thompson and three others continued on through the pass to the line shack, Longarm and the remaining riders, led by the old wrangler, followed a steep game trail skirting it.

High on the trail above the valley, Longarm paused to watch as Thompson and his men vanished into the pass. Then he waved to Sam, who pulled his horse around and continued to lead them to the crest of the butte. They followed the butte for some distance, coming at last to a trail cutting down through a flat covered with huge boulders. They kept on, skirting the boulders warily until they reached the far end of the flat and saw the line shack on a narrow ledge below them.

But it appeared that Longarm's posse was not going to be taking these gunslicks by surprise. Two of them were perched on a ledge above the shack, their rifles at the ready. It was a nearly impregnable position and gave them a perfect view of the slope below them. Where the third gunman was, Longarm had no idea. But he was down there somewhere, Longarm had no doubt.

Longarm dismounted, his own rifle in hand. Sam and the other two riders, cranking their rifles, dismounted and joined him. Abruptly, the two on the ledge opened up. Longarm heard the dim rattle of rifle fire coming from below. He hoped Thompson and his men were smart enough to leave their horses and take cover. There was no way they could ride up to the line shack in the teeth of that fire.

"Let's go," Longarm said to Sam and the other two. "We won't do much good standing here."

Longarm in the lead, the four men plunged down the slope. The footing was treacherous, the slope covered with gravel and slabs of shale. They were nearly at the foot of the slope when a warning cry came from the rear of the shack, followed by a fusillade coming at them from behind the shack, the rounds whining off the shale and sending the gravel flying.

Sam gasped in pain and went tumbling headlong past Longarm down the slope. When Longarm reached its bottom, he bent over Sam, caught him by the back of his vest, and dragged him behind some rocks. The other two men found shelter further up the slope and did their best to return the fire coming at them from the shack.

Peering out from behind a rock, Longarm saw that the two gunmen on the ledge had vanished.

He looked down the slope and saw Thompson and two other men clambering up it, their sixguns thundering. Abruptly, from the other side of the shack, three horsemen bolted, heading away from the shack. The rider in the lead wore a white hat and was dressed all in black.

Stepping out from cover, Longarm tracked the last rider and squeezed off a shot. His target, an older man who had been riding somewhat clumsily, flung up his hands and spun off his mount. The rider in front of him, a kid who couldn't be much more than twenty, spurred his horse back to his downed comrade. As Longarm fired on him, he reached down and hauled the wounded man up behind his saddle, wheeled his mount, and rode after the other one. By this time, Thompson and his men had reached Longarm. Though they added their own hail of lead to Longarm's, the fleeing gunmen were soon out of sight.

Longarm turned to Thompson and saw that the foreman had been hit in the left arm and was apparently in considerable pain, though he made no mention of it as he brushed past Longarm to bend over Sam.

"How bad is it, Sam?" he asked.

Sam looked up at Thompson, a bleak smile on his grizzled face. "Feels like he used a real bullet. And it's still in there."

"Where?"

Before he could reply, he began coughing and further questioning was not needed. As Sam slumped forward, his vest opened and everyone huddled around him could see the gaping hole in his chest. If the wound wasn't immediately fatal, it would be soon enough.

"Son of a bitch," said Longarm. "They were waiting for us. We didn't surprise them one bit."

Thompson nodded glumly. "That's the way it looks, all right."

"Take Sam back to the Circle T. Looks like both of you need help."

"What are you going to do?"

"I'm going after them. They've got a wounded man too, don't forget. They'll have to stop soon to tend to him."

"Why go after them alone?"

"I'll make less noise. Maybe I can surprise them."

"Good luck," Thompson said.

Glancing down at Thompson's hand, Longarm saw it was scarlet with his blood, the ground beneath it saturated. The man was losing entirely too much blood.

"You better bind up that wound before you ride back," Longarm told him. "Stop that bleeding."

"Yeah," said Thompson, sagging back onto a boulder, his face as white as a sheet, beads of cold sweat oozing out of his forehead. "I guess maybe I'd better."

Longarm left them and scrambled back up the slope to get to his horse.

"I'm tellin' you, Dutch. We got two of them," Studs insisted. "One comin' up the slope, that other one you got behind the shack. Right now, they're off lickin' their wounds."

"Maybe yes," said Dorfman. "Maybe no."

"We ain't been followed, I'm sure of it."

"Okay. We stay here then. Light a fire and take care of the old bastard. I'll be on guard up near that rock just in case."

They had ridden into a small arroyo, its sheer walls bending over them like protective wings. Gimpy was on the shaded ground, his head propped up on Studs's folded jacket. He had taken two slugs. The first one had struck his skull, entering over his left brow and exiting just behind his left ear, blowing out an inch-wide fragment of skull bone. The second slug had caught him in the back, knocking him out of his saddle. Both wounds were clean now, and Studs had stopped the bleeding with bandages he had made by ripping up one of the old man's shirts. Gimpy was fully conscious, but for the past half hour or so he had been complaining that he couldn't see and that he had no feeling in his right arm and leg. In addition, the old man couldn't seem to get warm; he shivered constantly.

Studs had a pretty good idea what these symptoms meant. The back wound was superficial, but the bullet which had passed through Gimpy's skull had sucked out some of his brain. If the old bastard survived, he would be a blind cripple. But Studs tried not to think of that as he built the fire.

Studs liked the old fart, and it didn't help any

for him to think what it would be like without him. Dutch was a cold son of a bitch, and at times Gimpy was an old woman, but of the two, he preferred Gimpy. If the poor bastard had ever learned how to make a decent cup of coffee, he'd have been the best damn cook Studs had ever ridden with.

The fire took hold. He fed more wood to it, and glanced up at the sky. Either it was clouding up or it was later than he thought.

"You any warmer, Gimpy?" he asked.

"Better," Gimpy said, "but I'm still cold. Build it up some more, will you?"

"Sure."

Studs continued to build the fire, and saw Gimpy's shivering finally come to a halt. Well, that was something. He leaned back against a boulder and built himself a cigarette.

Before he could light it, Gimpy grumbled, "What about me?"

"Sure," said Studs, placing the cigarette between Gimpy's lips and lighting it for him. As Studs made himself another smoke, Gimpy puffed on it fitfully.

"How you feelin' now?" he asked Gimpy.

"Better," he said. "Thanks, Studs."

"See if you can't get some sleep now you're warmer. We got a ways to go yet."

"I'm gettin' too old for this sort of thing. Soon's I get back on my feet, think mebbe I'll head on back to Texas."

"Good idea, Gimpy."

"Find myself a little spread with a porch."

"And maybe a rockin' chair?"

"Yeah." He took a few awkward puffs on the cigarette. "Say, Studs."

"What?"

"Would you . . . quit callin' me Gimpy?"

"What'll I call you?"

"My name's Winslow. Peter Winslow . . . ain't sech a bad name."

"No, it ain't, Pete."

He smiled. "That sounds better. It sure as hell does."

As he spoke, the cigarette fell from his mouth, and when Studs picked it up and tried to place it between the old man's lips, he found he could not do so.

Gimpy was dead.

"Dutch!" Studs called.

In a moment Dutch was crouching beside him, studying the old man's slack face.

"Shit," said Dutch. "That settles it."

"What do you mean?"

"I liked the old bastard. He took a lot of shit and he whined a lot, but he was a good buddy of my old man. That's why I looked out for him. Now he's dead and Levinson's the one caused it."

"You certain sure Levinson set us up for this?"

"As sure as I need to be."

"So, what do we do?"

"We make the son of a bitch pay, but first we got to bury Gimpy here."

"We ain't got no shovel."

Dutch looked around the narrow defile, then

pointed to a spot behind some boulders on the
other side. "We'll plant him over there, in among
those rocks. We'll pile some boulders on top of him,
so the coyotes can't get at him—or the vultures.
That's the best we can do."

"No marker?"

"No marker. My pa never had a marker neither.
Hell, that don't mean nothin'. Gimpy's marker'll
be the sky—and these here hills. C'mon, let's get
to it."

As Dutch lifted Gimpy's legs, Studs took Gimpy
under his shoulders and the two lugged him
across the ravine. As he carried the dead man,
Studs was struck by how light this frail old bird
had been. They waded ankle deep through the
icy stream that cut through the gorge, and when
they reached the rocks, eased Gimpy's body gently
down behind them. Despite what Dutch had said
a moment before, it seemed kind of cold-blooded;
but once the boulders had covered the dead man
completely, Studs realized that Dutch and he
were doing the right thing.

"Let's get out of here," said Dutch.

"We got a fire going. We could camp here for
the night."

"You crazy? We ain't camping here."

"Well, where we goin' to camp then?"

"Somewhere between here and the Jinglebob."

They saddled up their mounts, filled their can-
teens, then gave their horses a final lick at the
stream. With Dutch in the lead, they urged their
mounts up the steep trail leading out of the gorge.

They were halfway up when a lone rider nudged his mount out from behind a boulder and blocked their path, his Winchester trained on them.

"Hold it right there, gents."

Dutch reined in. "Who the hell are you, mister?"

"Name's Custis Long. Deputy U.S. marshal."

"You were with that posse?"

"I led it."

"Bastard."

"Unbuckle your gunbelts, real slow like, and let them drop to the ground."

Dutch's hand dropped to his belt, but instead of unbuckling it, he yanked his reins with cruel force. His horse reared back on his hind legs, his forelegs clawing at the air, his belly between Dutch and the marshal. Rolling back off the horse, Dutch drew his sixgun, and when he hit the ground, fired up at the marshal, then ran for cover behind some rocks. Before the marshal could fire back, Studs clapped spurs to his mount and drove it forward into the lawman's horse, knocking it to one side. With a fearful shriek, the horse slipped off the trail, then plunged headfirst down the slope, dragging its rider along with it. As Studs watched, both horse and rider disappeared into the ravine, their descent obscured by a roiling cloud of dust.

Studs calmed his horse with a few pats on its neck, then looked over at the rocks where Dutch had taken refuge.

"You all right, Dutch?" he called.

"Yeah," Dutch replied, standing up. "Nice going, Studs. That was quick thinking."

Dutch left the rocks and grabbed his horse's dangling reins, pulled the still-skittish animal around, and vaulted into the saddle. Without even a glance back, he continued on up the trail. Studs took one quick look down the slope, then spurred after Dutch.

When Brian rode into the Jinglebob compound, Clara was on the veranda in her wheelchair, a blanket over her lap. Standing in the middle of the yard was an open flatbed wagon, a tarpaulin flung over the coffin resting in it. Two swaybacked mares stood in the wagon's traces, their tails drooping in the hot noonday sun. As Brian dismounted in front of the veranda, his crew, Sim Bond in the lead, started for the house. It was plain they had been waiting some time for him—as had his mother.

"Where in tarnation you been?" she demanded.

"I had business."

"Business? Speak out, man. Where were you?"

"I was with Ruthanne Tremaine."

"You were at the Circle T?"

"You heard me."

"All night?"

"Why not?"

"I don't believe you. That woman has more sense than to cotton up to the likes of you."

Brian glanced over at the wagon. "How long has that been there?"

"Since last night. The undertaker's waiting for his fee. I had to send Sim in for Slope's body. Bury it."

"Right now? I'm hungry. Ain't had breakfast."

"She didn't feed you, huh?"

Brian turned on her in a sudden fury. "Damn you, witch! Shut the hell up or I'll throw you and that wheelchair down these steps and make you crawl back up!"

So livid was his fury, Clara jumped back in her chair, eyes widening in startled surprise. Brian swung around to the approaching members of his crew and fixed his foreman with blazing eyes. Sim pulled up, and the rest of the crew as well.

"Dammit, Sim," Brian said, "what in the hell are you doing leaving that wagon sitting there for? Get some men to drive that wagon out to the west pasture and plant Slope under one of them big pines. I'll be out after I've had breakfast."

Then he mounted the veranda steps, brushed past his mother, and went into the house. Carlotta's big figure was padding heavily down the hallway toward him.

"Ham and eggs, Carlotta," he told her, "and plenty of coffee. You got any fresh doughnuts?"

On her way back to the kitchen she looked back at him and nodded.

"I'll be on the veranda."

He turned, pushed open the door, and stepped back out onto the veranda, feeling surprisingly better, the depression he had experienced since the night before gone completely. As a matter of fact, he was just a little proud of himself, wondering now—even surprised—at his earlier regret for what he had had to do the night before. After all, in a sense, he had fired at that damn fool nester in self-defense. He had been facing a man with a loaded shotgun, after all. And now, as things were turning out, he was rid of the only witnesses to what he had done.

His mother was still on the veranda. He strode past her, waiting for her to make another remark about him and Ruthanne. He would take great pleasure in doing what he had threatened.

Sitting back in a rocker, he watched as the wagon, two of his cowhands up on the seat, left the yard on its way out to the west pasture.

Clara glanced over at him, her face rigid. "I told you," she said, her voice tight with fury, "that I didn't want to know where you buried him."

"I won't tell you which pine he's under."

"You bastard."

"That's no way for you to talk to your only surviving son," he told her.

"It's the way I prefer."

"Keep it up."

"And you'll do what?"

"Whatever it takes to shut you up."

His words were menacing enough to cause her to stare at him through suddenly wary eyes. He smiled back at her.

"My, my," she said. "What's got into you, Brian? You seem ready to eat your weight in wildcats." Then she released her venom. "Perhaps you did spend the night with that Tremaine whore after all."

Brian got up from his chair, grabbed the wheelchair's handles, and spun it brutally around. He leaned over Clara, pushed open the door, and flung her, chair and all, into the entrance hall. The wheelchair slammed into the foot of the stairs. Squealing like a stuck pig, Clara tumbled forward out of the wheelchair, landing awkwardly on the bottom stairs. Carlotta, padding down the hallway with Brian's breakfast, dodged nimbly aside and continued past him out onto the veranda.

He might have been mistaken, but it seemed to him that he caught a gleam of approval in the Indian woman's liquid black eyes.

Chapter 7

Longarm pulled the branch closer, then worked it carefully in under the boulder still pinning his right leg. Propping himself up on his left elbow, he lifted the branch slowly, carefully. For a moment it appeared the branch would crack under the stress; instead, the boulder eased back an inch or so. Gritting his teeth, Longarm turned his foot, raised the branch an inch more—then yanked his foot free.

The relief was extraordinary. He sat up and pulled the boot off his foot. It was swollen some and discolored, but nothing appeared to be broken. He eased himself upright and put his full weight on it. He could walk, but not very far at first, and not without a crutch of some kind. He settled on the branch he had just finished using. Fitting it under his right arm, he hobbled past the horse he had put out of its misery an hour ago.

There was a horse left behind at the line shack, he remembered. It belonged to that gunslick he had shot out of his saddle. His best chance was to head back along the trail he had followed until he reached the line shack.

It was dark when he finally did. It had been a long, weary journey, and by the time he reached the shack he was limping painfully. The horse was there, as he had surmised. It was behind the shack, still saddled, cropping the grass still left in the shade. Longarm decided to rest up, and after refreshing himself at the spring behind the shack, slept the night through inside it. He got up early the next morning and headed back to the Circle T.

Sam was still alive when he reached the Circle T the day before, but he was in such poor condition he was unable to practice on himself the same skills he'd used on Eben, and there was little that could be done for him, especially since he would not allow anyone to ride into town after the doctor. He insisted on being brought out to his room in the barn, and there he remained with a bottle of whiskey to keep his spirits up and kill the pain.

Jim Thompson's wound was taken care of in the bunkhouse, where he insisted on staying. Like Sam, he realized that with Eben Heath still in poor condition in the ranch house's living room, their presence would only cause still more confusion. The round had torn up Thompson's arm pretty well, but no bones were broken; all that was required was to keep the wound clean and staunch the bleeding. This Ruthanne accomplished without too much difficulty.

Now she was cutting carefully through Jim's bandage to inspect his wound. She brightened considerably when she saw that it was not festering. The torn flesh was not puffy and some of the swelling had gone down. She made a fresh compress and bandaged the arm tightly once more.

This accomplished, she sank wearily into a chair beside Jim's cot.

"I'm afraid the Circle T is becoming a hospital ward," she said. "It smells of carbolic acid and alcohol."

Jim smiled at her. "I know what you mean. For myself, I prefer the smell of fresh coffee."

"Maybe we'll return to that someday—when this terrible business is over."

"I hope so. By the way, how's Sam?"

"I looked in on him before I came in here. He's making good use of that whiskey."

"Ruthanne, I'm worried about that deputy marshal."

"Custis?"

"Yeah. It's past noon. He's been gone all night. He should be back by now."

Jim had given Ruthanne a vivid description of the firefight at the line shack, and she knew that

117

Custis had gone after two of Brian's gunslicks on his own. "I'm sure he'll be all right," she assured Jim. "After all, this is his line of work, isn't it?"

"Maybe so," Jim said, "but I think I'd better go after him."

"But you can't. You lost so much blood. A bed sheet has more color than you have."

"What difference does that make? We can't leave him out there alone."

"It's a choice he made himself, Jim," she reminded him firmly.

"You don't want me to go?"

"Of course not. I want you to stay here and get some rest."

"Yes, ma'am," he said, grinning.

Their eyes met, and in that instant Ruthanne almost reached out to take Jim's hand. She had to remind herself that Jim Thompson was her foreman. What she had told Longarm still held. No cattlewoman could allow intimacy with her foreman without a ruinous loss of control over her operation. And this spread was all she had.

Jim sensed her pulling back. She saw it in his eyes. For that she was sorry. But there was no help for it, she concluded.

"It's that U.S. deputy, isn't it," he said.

"What do you mean?"

"You like him."

"Why, Jim, that's . . . impertinent!"

He looked away, his strong, handsome face set. "Yes, I suppose it is. I'm sorry, Mrs. Tremaine."

"Now, I do prefer Ruthanne, Jim,"

But her words did not put that warmth back in his eyes. For that, she supposed, she should be grateful. She leaned back in the chair for a moment, studying him, her heart in a strange turmoil as she saw him staring straight ahead now, resolute in his determination not to breach the wall separating the owner of the Circle T from the hired help.

She got to her feet. "I'll be in later, Jim," she said. "You try to get some rest now. Okay?"

"Okay," he said.

Outside in the brilliant sunshine Ruthanne found herself mulling over what Jim had said. Was he right? Did she like Custis that way? A sudden apprehension fell over her then. She shaded her eyes and peered in the direction of North Canyon.

Where *was* Custis?

Brian's two cowhands, Deke and Bill, had already buried Slope when Brian reached the pines and dismounted. He walked over and nodded to his two hands, who were leaning on their shovels now, watching him curiously. This was obviously not the sort of burial they had expected for the brother of the Jinglebob's owner.

Brian glanced at the low mound of moist earth covering Slope's remains. It was difficult for him to contain his elation. The death of Eben Heath and the end of his thrall to those three gunslicks put him now firmly in charge of his destiny. He thought of his mother then. Carried upstairs by

Carlotta, wheelchair and all, she was in her room now, sobbing out her rage and frustration, beaten thoroughly for the first time in her life.

"Pound the dirt down," Brian told the two hands. "Then dig up squares of sod and place them over the spot. After that, spread grass seed over the grave site."

"We don't have no grass seed," protested Deke.

"I guess maybe we don't, at that. Well, I'll be going into town later today. I'll pick some up at the feed store."

The two men proceeded to stamp on the ground as ordered. To Brian, they seemed comically solemn as they stomped around on the small rectangular mound, slowly but steadily beating the mound down.

Brian stepped back up onto his horse and rode down the slope to the compound, where he told Sim to select four riders and saddle up, that they were heading into town.

It was mid-afternoon when the six men nudged their horses over to the hitch rack in front of the Cattleman's Rest. Brian pushed his way through the batwings and looked about him in pleased astonishment at how crowded his place was this early in the day.

The saloon went suddenly quiet as Brian and his five cowhands crowded through the doorway. Brian's men were weary from the long ride, a thin patina of dust covering their hats and shoulders. Brian led the way to the bar. Those patrons already at the bar moved swiftly aside.

"Howdy, Ben," Brian said to the barkeep, the man who managed the place for him.

"Howdy, Boss. Good to see you."

"Business looks good."

"Yeah, it sure is," Ben replied, somewhat nervously.

"Whiskey," Brian told him. Then he glanced down the bar at the patrons crowding it. "All around. I'm payin'."

That loosened things up considerably, and after the drinks were passed out, the hubbub returned to normal. Brian left his ranch hands, took his glass over to a table along the wall, and beckoned Ben over so they could talk. Ben ducked out from under his apron, lifted the bar flap, and hurried over to join Brian.

"Ben," Brian said, as soon as his saloon manager sat down, "how come we're doin' so good?"

"Didn't you hear? Meg O'Riley's closed the The Drover's Home. Bull's dead."

"Since when?"

"Since last night. The funeral's over already."

"Good. I won't have to attend."

"He was beat up pretty bad, Brian. People sure don't like what happened to Bull—or to Meg O'Riley either."

"That so? What *did* happen?"

"Three riders came in and beat the shit out of Bull, then went upstairs and raped Meg." He swallowed nervously. "There's some say you know who did it."

"Some say? Who, Ben?"

"Meg."

Brian laughed. "Now who in the hell is going to believe that whore? Why, Ben, I ain't got the foggiest notion who'd do such a terrible thing. By the way, where's Seth and Cal? When I rode past the sheriff's office, it was locked up."

"Didn't you hear?"

"If I heard, for Christ's sake, would I be asking?"

"That deputy U.S. marshal who came for that prisoner kicked them out of town. Now Meg's convinced Bill Grant to convene a council meeting tonight. Word is they're going to create a town marshal job and give it to that U.S. deputy marshal."

"That so? Where the hell is this deputy marshal? He's up here throwing weight around, and I ain't even met him yet."

Ben shrugged. "I don't know where he is either, Boss."

Brian smiled and leaned back to sip his whiskey. "Well, I wouldn't worry none about him."

The barkeep glanced quickly at Brian, then frowned. "Hey, you mean he's out of it?"

"Thanks, Ben. You can go on back to the bar now."

"Sure thing, Boss."

Brian watched the man push his way through the double ranks of patrons still crowding the bar, then got up, left the saloon, and continued on down Main Street until he came to Bill Grant's feed mill.

He found Bill Grant in back, sending some grain down a chute, the air filled with tiny, gleaming dust motes. Bill was a squat, heavy man with beetling brows and thick hair. At the moment it was almost completely gray from flour dust. When he saw Brian, he closed the chute, ran his hand nervously through his hair, and walked toward him, a forced smile on his face.

Brian turned about and led the way to Bill's glassed-in office up front. He waited outside politely for Bill to open the door and go in ahead of him, then followed him inside and sat down in the wooden chair by his desk.

"What can I do for you, Brian?" Bill asked.

"Hear we got a meeting of the town council tonight."

"Yeah, that's right."

"I didn't know anything about it."

"You didn't? Why, that's queer, Brian. I thought everyone in town knew."

"I'm not in town, Bill. I got a spread outside, the Jinglebob. Remember?"

"Well, I sure hope you didn't think we were planning on convening a town council without its president on hand."

"I admit, that sure would be strange."

"Like I said, we wouldn't think of doing such a thing."

"It would be dangerous," Brian continued relentlessly. "Downright dangerous."

"See here, Brian. You threatening me?"

Brian leaned forward in his chair. "How long

do you think it would take for you to call off this council meeting, Bill?"

Bill Grant moistened his lips. "I couldn't do that, Brian. We got everyone all set for it."

"That so?"

"Brian, we ain't got no law left in this town, what with the sheriff dead and them two deputies lighting out."

"So you're going to hire that federal marshal."

"I told you. We need law."

"You got law. Me. And the election's only a week off. Just be patient, Bill, and this here town'll have all the law it wants and needs."

"It's just . . . well, it's a good idea to have some-one until then, don't you think?"

"Why?"

Bill stirred uneasily under Brian's stare.

"I'm waiting, Bill."

"Bad things been happenin'," he said dogged-ly.

"What things?"

"Bull Danham's been killed and Meg O'Riley's been raped."

"I heard all about it. Someone took a pool cue to Bull, and that whore had to give it away for a change. You call that bad?"

"That ain't all. There's some people suspicious about the way the sheriff died."

"He got blown up. It was an accident."

"Some say it wasn't."

"Who says it wasn't?"

He moistened his lips again. "Meg."

124

Brian sat back in the chair. "Cancel the council meeting, Bill. I don't want another one this soon. Later maybe, after the election."

He got up then and left the office, closing the door softly as he glanced in through the glass. A very unhappy Bill Grant stared back at him.

Out on the sidewalk, the warm sunlight baking his face, he strode along feeling just fine. He was catching up, nipping trouble in the bud, riding a crest. He thought of Ruthanne then. Why should he allow himself to give up on her so soon? Be patient, he counseled himself. Who knows what the future might bring.

He came to The Drover's Home, mounted the porch steps, and pushed through the batwings into the darkened saloon. The place smelled sour, looked abandoned. The sawdust on the floor was filthy; the spittoons had not been emptied and were filled to the brim, tobacco juice stains covering the floor around them.

He halted in the middle of the place. "Meg!" he called.

Almost instantly, as if she had been waiting for his summons, a door was flung open at the far end of the room and Meg appeared in the doorway. She was dressed in a long nightgown, her hair in disarray. She looked terrible. For a crazy moment he thought she was actually in mourning for the man she had cuckolded so easily.

"I come to talk to you, Meg."

"I don't have to talk to you, Brian. Get out of my place."

"Well, now, that ain't so, is it?"

"What do you mean?"

"This here ain't your place. It was Bull had the license. You just went along for the ride. Ain't that so?"

"It was an arrangement, yes."

"So now Bull's gone—and so is the arrangement."

"I'll get a license myself now," she said, just the hint of fear in her voice. "You can't take this place from me."

"You ain't hearin' right. This saloon ain't yours to begin with."

"But I gave Bull the money he needed to buy it, and for the liquor license. Everyone knows that."

"And he was your husband. Everyone knew that—except you."

"What are you tryin' to say."

"That when the council meets—after I'm sheriff—we'll give your application due consideration, then turn it down. We don't need your kind in this town, Meg. You stink it up."

"You mean that, don't you."

"Yes."

She stood there looking at him, seeming to sway in the doorway.

"Oh, one more thing," he went on. "If you think that U.S. deputy is going to help you, think again. He's out of it."

"I don't believe you."

"Then don't. By the way, I got Bill Grant to call off the council meeting for tonight. No sense in

126

having one until I become sheriff."

He turned on his heels and strode from the
saloon. He was descending the porch when he
heard Meg's slippered feet running across the saloon floor. When she burst through the batwings,
he was in the street. He turned. She had a foolish little pepperbox in her hand. He watched in
astonishment as she fired at him. The tiny bullets
kicked up a storm at his feet. Then one caught
his sleeve. Without thinking, he drew his sixgun
and fired at her point blank. When she continued
to fire at him, he shot again, and this time his
bullet caught her in the belly. She knifed over and
plunged forward down the steps into the street.

Townsmen came running. Meg's first shots had
brought people streaming out onto the sidewalks.
Everyone had seen her firing at Brian. He had
shot at her in self-defense. But for him, it didn't
seem to help. He holstered his weapon and pushed
hurriedly through the crowd, heading for the Cattleman's Rest. He needed another whiskey.

About an hour later, when the excitement
surrounding Meg's death had abated somewhat,
Brian sent over money to the undertaker so he
could bury Meg in some style. Then he and his
men left the Cattleman's Rest and rode out, leaving behind a sober, uneasy town.

Longarm was sure now. The rider approaching
him astride a handsome black was Ruthanne. She
was wearing Levi's, checked shirt, vest, and a
Stetson. But there was sure as hell no mistaking

her for a man. When she saw him, she stood up in her stirrups and waved. He waved back.

"My God, Custis," she said when they pulled alongside each other. "You look awful."

"Maybe you can guess how I feel then."

"What happened?"

"I spent some time under a mountain. It's a long story. Let's just say I wasn't too successful bringing in them two remaining gunslicks."

"Remaining?"

"There were only two of them when I made my move. How're Thompson and the wrangler?"

"Jim's going to be all right, I think. But I'm not so sure about Sam. He needs to have that bullet taken out of his chest—only he refuses to go into town and see the doc."

"Maybe we'll have to talk him into it."

"You can't do that. He won't let that alcoholic quack get near him."

"He won't have any choice. I'll put him in a wagon and take him in. I got business in town anyway."

"But he won't go."

"I'll tie him down if I have to."

"Well, maybe that's best, at that."

"It was nice of you to ride out after me."

She glanced quickly at him. "I was worried."

"For a while there, so was I."

"You sure you're all right?"

"I'm fine—a little beaten up maybe, but still fit to handle what's ahead."

"And after you have done that?"

"If I'm still healthy, I'll be on my way back to Denver."

"You wouldn't . . . consider staying here?"

They rode on for a while without Longarm replying. Then he looked over at her. "You mean with you?"

"Do I have to spell it out for you, Custis?"

"No, you don't. And I admit, it's tempting. This is fine country. And you're some fine-looking gal."

"But that's not enough to make you stay. Is that it?"

"Afraid so." He smiled. "Don't feel bad. It's got nothing to do with you. It's me. I'm not the marrying kind, and I can't see myself playing nursemaid to a bunch of bawling cattle for the rest of my life."

"No, I guess you wouldn't like that."

"I hazed cattle in younger, more foolish days. What I found was it's a job for rubber bones and younger, resilient muscles. I'm beginning to creak some, I noticed." He glanced at her. "What about this Jim Thompson, your foreman?"

"I told you."

"He's the foreman and you're the boss—a mix that won't work?"

"Yes. But there's something else as well. I was thinking about it while I was riding out, looking for you."

"What's that?"

"You and I spent the night together. And Jim knows that."

"I see what you mean. That could be a problem."

"Yes."

They rode on a ways in silence. Then he glanced at her. "If you play your cards right, Ruthanne, it need not be a problem."

She reined in the black and looked over at him. "I'm listening."

"I was careful when I came downstairs. You were busy heating water at the stove and didn't see me. When I entered the living room where Eben was, I came in from the sitting room across the hall."

"Why's that so important?"

"It means you can insist to Jim that I slept downstairs. As long as you keep to that story, there's no way he can refute it."

"But Longarm. That would be lying."

"A lie that would make it very easy for Jim to forget about me. As long as you keep to that story, you'll soon believe it yourself. Just one thing. Never tell Jim the truth. That would be needlessly cruel."

"Then I must live with that lie for the rest of my life?"

"Is that too high a price to pay to let Jim keep his pride—and let you keep a husband at your side who loves you?"

"I guess not."

"Good. It's settled then."

She laughed. "Custis! Nothing's settled. Jim hasn't even asked me."

"I get the feeling he will, if you give him the chance."

130

• • •

Jim Thompson was standing in front of the bunkhouse when they rode in, his wounded left arm in a sling. He walked up to greet them, and taking hold of the bridle to Ruthanne's black, held it while she dismounted.

"I see you found him," he remarked.

"She did that," Longarm told him, dismounting. "And she brought me back all safe and sound."

"Maybe so. But you don't look so good."

"How do you feel?"

"Weak, but I'm on the mend."

"Ruthanne said Sam won't go into town to get that bullet taken out."

"He doesn't trust the town doc."

"Maybe I'd better forget what he wants and take him in anyway."

"Against his will? He'll put up a ruckus."

"If you've got a wagon I can use, I'll take him in right now. I got business in town."

Ruthanne spoke up then. "I think we should, Jim. We can't just let Sam stay in that barn until he dies."

"It's what he wants."

"It's not what I want."

"And you're the boss, I suppose."

"Yes, Jim. I'm the boss. If you want to put it that way."

"Is there any other way for me to put it?"

Longarm could see the steam building between the two, and quickly led his horse past them to the barn. Once inside, he unsaddled the mount and backed it into a stall, then brought the thirsty animal a fresh bucket of water. The horse bore a Jinglebob brand, and Longarm had every intention of returning it when the dust settled.

He entered Sam's room. The old wrangler was flat on his back on his cot, a whiskey bottle clutched in one hand. He turned his head and stared blearily up at Longarm. He looked bad, very bad. His old eyes had a feverish, hectic glow to him.

"You got back, hey?"

"I'm back. Finish that bottle and brace yourself."

"Why?"

"I'm taking you into town."

"To see that quack?"

"Yep, unless you want Ruthanne to bury you. She likes you, Sam. It wouldn't do her any good to have to go through something like that. I ain't thinking of you. It's her I'm worried about."

"Now, listen here—"

But Longarm didn't have time to listen. He turned and left the old man to utter any further protest at a closed door.

Chapter 8

It was close to dusk when Longarm pulled the wagon to a halt in front of the doctor's office, a small ramshackle affair shoehorned in between a haberdashery and a saddle shop. He jumped down from the wagon seat and knocked on the office door. When he got no response, he peered in through a window. The office appeared to be empty.

"You lookin' for the doc?" a passerby asked.

Longarm turned. "Yeah. Where the hell is he? I got a very sick man in that wagon."

"He's over at the Cattleman's Rest." The townsman was a potbellied fellow sporting a yellow checked vest and a bowler hat. He chuckled. "You better get over there fast, he's really puttin' one on."

"Do me a favor," said Longarm. "Watch Sam there in the wagon while I get the doc."

The townsman had no chance to protest as Longarm strode past him across the wide main street to the Cattleman's Rest. He burst through the batwings and came to a halt as he surveyed the place. It was strangely quiet. The few patrons at the bar turned to gaze at him. Then they went back to their drinks, almost dutifully, without much apparent pleasure.

The doc was at a table in a far corner, his head resting on his folded arms, a bottle on the table before him. Longarm strode across the saloon and, reaching the doc's table, yanked his head up. The doc blinked blearily up at him.

"What d'you want?" he muttered.

"I need your services."

"Later. I ain't fit. See me tomorrow."

Longarm hauled the doc out of his chair, draped him over his shoulder, and carried him from the saloon. When he reached the doc's office, he brushed past the townsman standing by the wagon and let the doc slam to the floor of the low porch. Kicking open the office door, he took hold of the doc's collar and dragged him inside, after which he lit a lamp sitting on his desk.

He stepped over the dazed physician then and went back out to carry Sam into his office. He put the unconscious man down on a cot along the wall and lit another lamp to give the doctor more light. As the lamp flared, Sam's eyes flickered open.

"We got here, did we?" he muttered faintly.

"Yep."

"Won't do no good."

"We'll see about that."

"Where's my bottle?"

"You finished it."

Longarm turned to look at the doc, who had both hands braced on his desk as he swayed over it. Longarm walked over to him.

"I'm tellin' you," the doc whined. "I ain't fit."

"Now you listen to me, Doc. You're going to take a bullet out of Sam's chest. If you don't, I promise—you'll never be fit again."

Longarm left him and stepped out onto the porch. The office door had been left open and a small crowd had gathered, most of them from the saloon he had just left. The townsman in the bowler hat was up on the porch, peering in at the doc and Sam.

"Get some coffee," Longarm told him. "Black coffee and plenty of it."

He was off without hesitation, heading for a restaurant down the street. Two others broke from the crowd to join him. Longarm got back up on the wagon's seat, released the brake, and drove the team down the street to the livery. He gave the hostler enough to take care of the horses and walked back to the doc's office. The crowd, much larger now, had moved closer.

"That Sam Waller in there?" someone called out to him. "From the Circle T?"

Longarm paused, his hand on the doorknob. "It's him, all right."

"What happened?"

"One of Brian Levinson's gunslicks put a round in his chest."

"Levinson?"

"You heard me."

An angry mutter swept the crowd.

The coffee arrived, two of the men carrying cups, the third a full coffee pot. Longarm opened the door for them, followed them into the office, and slammed the door shut. He pushed the doc down into his chair and shoved a cup of coffee at him.

"Drink up!"

With quavering hands, the doc lifted the closest cup to his lips and began swallowing. "It's hot!" he complained.

"Keep drinking!"

The doc gulped two cups down. Longarm refilled them, and he drank those. When Longarm poured another round, the doc took one look at the cups of steaming black liquid and ran out into the back alley and threw up his guts. He returned then, wiping off his mouth with the back of his hands, and waved Longarm off as he began preparing himself for the operation.

Longarm peered at him closely. "You goin' to be all right, Doc?"

"Yes, you bastard. Now get out of here and let me work."

"You won't need any help?"

"See if Cass Winfield's out there."

Longarm opened the door and stepped out onto

the porch. "Cass Winfield around?"

"What d'you want?"

"Doc needs you."

The man pushed through the crowd, brushed past Longarm, and disappeared inside. Longarm took a deep breath. The doc was a lush, but when he was sober, he seemed to know his business. For the first time he felt hopeful about Sam.

He looked around the crowd. "Which way's Bill Grant's feed mill?"

"That's me. What do you want me for?"

Longarm looked over to see a chunky fellow with a round, beefy face pushing toward him through the crowd.

"You Bill Grant?"

"I just told you I was."

"Did Meg get to see you yet?"

"About what?"

"Convening the town council."

Grant pulled up in front of him. The crowd had become uncannily quiet, as if every man there had pulled in his breath at the same time. "You don't know then."

"What should I know?"

"Meg O'Riley's dead. We just got through burying her."

In the restaurant, coffee in front of him, Longarm listened while Grant told him about the one-sided gunfight.

"Everyone saw what happened," Grant concluded. "Meg shot first."

137

"With a silly little belly gun."

"Brian waited—until it looked like she winged him. Then he began firing back at her."

"So, legally, it's self-defense."

"No question about it."

"What set Meg off?"

"I don't know for sure. Brian was in the saloon with her for a while, and when he left she came after him and began firing. I figure he warned her about this upcoming council meeting. Warned her, then threatened her. So she came after him."

"What did he have over her?"

"Her saloon license. He has enough power to prevent her from getting one. That's why she had to marry Bull in the first place, to get an operating license. The marriage was just a dodge. Everyone knew that."

"So Levinson went in there to tell her that there'd be no council meeting or he'd put her out of business."

Grant nodded. "That's the way I see it. Earlier, he did not hesitate to threaten me. And there's something else."

"What?"

"Levinson's changed. He's meaner, more sure of himself—like he's been smoking some pretty potent stuff lately."

"Maybe he has," Longarm replied grimly.

He got up, dropped a coin on the table for his coffee, and left the place, Grant coming with him. The crowd, much bigger now, had moved up onto the doc's porch. Those townsmen in the front ranks were peering in through the windows, giving reports back to the others.

Longarm bulled his way onto the porch, then pushed back the crowd. Reluctantly, they retreated until most of them were standing in the street. Then he held up his hands to quiet them.

"How many here from the town council?" he asked.

A few hands shot up. Turning to his right, he saw Grant's hand go up as well. In all, he counted seven council members present.

"Grant, we got enough here?"

"You mean for a meeting?"

"That's what I mean."

"It's a quorum, yeah."

"Then we'll have that town council meeting right here."

"Who says?" someone cried.

"I say. And Grant here is going to make it legal. He's the secretary, and he'll put it all down. That right, Grant?"

Somewhat reluctantly, Grant nodded.

Then Longarm addressed the crowd and its council members. "I want you gents to make me the town marshal, with jurisdiction at least twenty miles outside the town in all directions."

"Why should we?" someone shouted.

"You don't have any law here now. And I'm a deputy U.S. marshal."

"Brian Levinson's the president of the council. He won't like this," someone else muttered.

"Why do you care, mister?" Longarm replied. "He's running roughshod over this town."

"If you mean Meg, she shot first. I saw it myself."

"What about Bull?"

"Three strangers rode in and did that."

"They were Brian's men."

"You can't prove that. I never saw none of them in here with Brian's crew. They was strangers."

"Brian hired them special and kept them hid in a line shack in North Canyon. It was one of them that wounded Sam Waller in there."

"I still say you can't prove nothing."

Longarm wanted that. He needed someone to present Levinson's side of the story so he could end all discussion with what he had. "I have an eyewitness who will prove that he shot Eben Heath down in cold blood."

"That sodbuster?"

"Yes."

There was a hush. Everyone in the crowd knew how Levinson felt about nesters, Eben Heath in particular.

"Who's your eyewitness?"

"Eben Heath. And his wife."

There was a shocked pause, then someone else cried, "Eben's not dead?"

"He's close to it, but there's a good chance now that he'll survive to testify in court. Levinson and those three riders I mentioned burned his barn down, then tried to burn Eben with it. His wife went into the barn and dragged him out."

Again there was silence as the crowd—and the members of the Pine Hill town council—digested this news.

"Now," Longarm said. "I want a vote making me town constable."

"There has to be a motion," Grant reminded Longarm.

"Make it then."

Grant so moved, asked for discussion. There was none. Someone shouted for the vote to be taken. When it was, every hand in the crowd shot up. There was safety in numbers, it seemed.

Grant looked over at Longarm. "I guess that does it, Mr. Long. You're now the town constable."

Longarm looked out over the crowd.

"All right, I need deputies," he said.

Two men stepped forward.

Longarm glanced over at Bill Grant. "What about you, Grant?"

"Don't count on me, Long. I've already put my neck out. Besides, I ain't much good with a gun. I'd likely blow my leg off if I tried to draw in anger."

Longarm looked at the two men. He was not impressed, but if this was all the help he was going to get, it would have to do. At least for now.

"Come see me first thing in the morning," he told them.

They nodded and strode off.

Longarm went back inside the doctor's office. Cass Winfield had left, but the doc was asleep, face down on the desk, the bent and flattened slug he had taken out of Sam's chest in front of him. Sam was asleep also, his breathing deep and steady, a bottle of whiskey provided by the doctor clutched in one hand.

Longarm left the office and closed the door behind him. Bill Grant was waiting for him with a key, the key to the sheriff's office. Longarm took it from him. Grant bid him good night and left. Longarm walked down the street to the sheriff's office, opened it, and lit a lamp. He slumped into the swivel chair, tried some drawers, and found the sheriff's badge, all polished and gleaming, resting in the top drawer under the blotter. He took it out and examined it, thought about the old lawman who had worn it so long, then pinned it on his shirt. He spun the swivel chair about once, crossed his legs, and rested his feet on the corner of the desk.

After a while his tailbone began to protest. He guessed he preferred a saddle and pulled his feet down. It was well into night by this time, the town was quiet—exhausted would probably be a better word—and the new town constable of Pine Hill was a very tired man. He remembered the hotel room he had taken when he got in and decided to take advantage of it. He blew out the lamp, locked the office door, and crossed the street to the hotel.

As he entered his room a few minutes later, he heard the sudden clatter of hoofbeats from the alley below. He went to the window and watched a lone rider gallop out of town to disappear in the direction of Brian Levinson's Jinglebob.

Longarm cocked an eyebrow and walked over to his dresser. He opened all the drawers and took out the newspapers lining them, crumpled the newsprint into balls, and dropped them on the floor in front of the door and around his bed. Then he shrugged out of his vest and sitting down on the bed, pulled off his boots. He hung his cross-draw rig on the bedpost, took out the .44—40 and slipped it under his pillow, snugged his derringer under his belt, and lay back and dropped his head on the pillow.

He was asleep instantly.

Brian was awake before Carlotta reached his bed. He sat up, scratching his head as he squinted at the sudden glare of the lamp she carried.

"What is this, Carlotta? It's the middle of the night."

"Juan is downstairs. He say he must speak to you."

"Juan? Your old man. He back?"

She nodded.

"What the hell's he want?"

"He say he must warn you. He say you got big trouble."

"Tell him he's full of shit."

Carlotta shrugged massively, then turned and headed for the door.

"No, dammit, wait a minute. Tell the redskin I'll see him on the porch."

Carlotta left his room.

Dressed in his robe, but not yet fully awake and irritated greatly by this late night alarm, Brian stepped out onto the veranda. The Indian was standing in front of a porch post, his arms folded, his anthracite eyes gleaming in the moonlight. He was Carlotta's husband, but he did not like living at the ranch with her paying his way. So he came and went as casual as the wind and Carlotta did not seem to mind.

Slumping back down into his rocker, Brian said, "Okay, what's all this about, Juan? And it better be good."

"I just come from town."

"So?"

"They got town constable now."

"What's that you say?"

Juan explained about the impromptu town council meeting in front of the doc's office, telling Brian everything he had seen and heard, including the U.S. deputy's assertion that Brian had shot down the nester and burned his place. When he went on to say that the nester was still alive, willing to testify against him, Brian sat up in sudden alarm. How in hell could that nester still be alive after he had planted two bullets in his chest?

Brian's thoughts raced. "Juan, you say this U.S. marshal brought in Sam Waller from the Circle T?"

"Sam was hurt bad. This marshal come into saloon and drag Doc out so he fix Sam."

"Did he say where the wounded nester was?"

144

Juan shook his head.

"Wake up the men in the bunkhouse, Juan, and get my chestnut saddled."

Brian watched the Indian disappear in the direction of the bunkhouse. He had a queasy feeling all of a sudden, as if the ground was shifting under him. It wasn't going the way it should. But he still had a chance. Silence this damned U.S. deputy. Then make a deal with that damn nester.

He was almost certain where the nester was. His homestead was close by the Circle T. It made sense for him to head for Ruthanne's place after Brian's attack. Of course, this meant it was all over now between him and Ruthanne. Well, so be it. For a moment he wished those gunslicks he'd brought up here were still siding him, but the fact that the marshal had returned safely from his attack on his line shack meant that they were either dead or in full flight. Either way suited him just fine.

Meanwhile, first things first.

He started for the front door. Before he reached it, his mother rolled out onto the porch and pulled her wheelchair around to block his way, her face gaunt in the moonlight, her eyes bright with malice.

"What have you done, Brian?"

"Nothing. Get out of my way."

"I heard Juan. Everything he said. You tried to kill that nester and bungled it."

"Get out of my way."

145

"That Tremaine whore's keeping the nester, ain't she—so he can testify against you."

"Get out of my way, I said."

"And now the U.S. marshal is getting ready to come after you. He was here before, looking for Sim—and for you too, I suspect. He strode right up onto this porch and took my shotgun out of my hands. He emptied it and rode off without looking back."

"You didn't tell me."

"He's a dangerous man, Brian."

"You worried about me?"

She laughed scornfully. "Worried? My God, no. Pleased. This U.S. marshal is more than a match for you."

"And that pleases you?"

"It does."

"But why? You're my mother."

"Don't remind me. I'd rather forget."

"You *are* a witch."

"If I were," she snapped bitterly, "you would have been dead long before this!"

"Dammit, Ma, you been after me ever since I can remember. Why?"

"Because you remind me of your father."

"Pa?"

"Pa was not your father. And Slope was not your half brother. The animal who sired him sired you as well. My first husband. I thought you would be different, so I took you with me when I left him. Pa legally adopted you, but it was all a terrible mistake. I see that now. You can't change your

146

fate. You are Slope all over again—and just as vicious, just as loathesome as that animal I left so long ago."

Clara's words were a revelation—an explanation finally for the implacable hatred she had shown toward him all these years. He swallowed hard and stared bitterly down at her.

"You're forgetting something," he said.

"I forget nothing."

"You forget it took two to create Slope and me. *Two*. You and my father. If I'm as rotten as my father, then you are as much to blame as he is." He leaned close to her, fixing her terrible eyes with his. "Behold, Mother, Slope and I are the results of your lust!"

She bent forward, her gnarled fingers pumping on the wheel, and with her head down, charged into him. He was knocked back, the wheelchair's frame slamming painfully into his stocking feet. He regained his balance and reaching out, spun her wheelchair around, then ran it off the porch, spilling her off the steps into the darkness.

For a moment or two, still seething, he listened to her curses, then strode into the house to get dressed.

Chapter 9

The Jinglebob riders made their entrance into
Pine Hill silently, on foot with their horses trail-
ing behind them. Brian led them into the alley
back of the hotel. When they reached the hotel,
they pulled up and with Brian, Sim Bond, and
Lundstrom leading the way, pulled open the back
door and entered. They proceeded down the dimly
lit hallway on cat feet, and found the desk clerk
asleep on a cot in his office behind the desk.

Brian skirted the desk and shook the clerk
awake. The clerk opened his eyes to find himself peering into the bore of Brian's revolver. He
began to sweat almost immediately.

"What room's that U.S. deputy marshal stayin'
in?"

"I . . . I don't know if he's up there!"

"I didn't ask you that. What's his room number?"

The clerk got up from the cot, took the spare room key from Longarm's letter box, and almost threw it at Brian. Brian caught it, glanced at the room number wired to it, then went back around the desk.

"Keep an eye on this one," he said to Lundstrom.

He motioned to Sim Bond and started up the stairs. The third-floor hallway was lit only feebly by wall lamps burning low to save kerosene. They found the correct room number nevertheless, and once outside the room Brian pressed his ear against the door. From within came the sound of steady breathing. He holstered his gun and inserted the key carefully, silently, and turned it, his left hand on the doorknob. Turning the doorknob, he pressed against the door and swung it open. Then he stepped back out of the doorway and glanced at Sim.

His sixgun out, Sim stepped carefully past him into the room. Drawing his own gun, Brian moved in behind him. There was a funny, scraping sound on the floor as his boot kicked something light. He cursed under his breath as Sim's boot did the same thing.

They were moving toward the bed and Brian could see the deputy's dark shape on it.

"Marshal," Brian barked harshly. "Lay still. I want to talk."

"So talk."

"You killed my brother."

"He came at me. I had no choice."

"I'm willing to grant that. I'm willing to let bygones be bygones. That prisoner you came for is gone, got blown up. Ain't no reason for you to stay on here. Take the train out tomorrow."

"And if I don't."

"I got a gun leveled on you, and so has Sim here."

"You kill me and you'll hang."

"I'll hang anyway if I let you live."

"No deals."

"Get him!" Levinson told Sim.

Abruptly the dark form on the bed exploded, fire lancing toward them. Brian heard Sim gasp as the weapon in his hand detonated. The deputy dove behind the bed, his sixgun thundering. Brian ducked low and fired back wildly, then bolted from the room, Sim staggering after him. Outside the door, Sim sprawled headlong.

Furious, Brian reached up for one of the lamps and flung it through the still-open door. A soft explosion followed and at once flames billowed in the room. He saw the deputy run for the door to escape and sent a fusillade of bullets at him. The man ducked back. The flames leaped higher, sending a fierce, glowing light into the hallway.

Again the deputy tried to bolt from the room, and again Brian's murderous fire sent him reeling back into the inferno. By now smoke was pouring out of the room, and the searing heat from the flames caused him to retreat back down the

151

hallway. Sim, barely visible now as the smoke blanketed him, remained facedown on the carpet. He was only a few feet from the blazing doorway, but lay without moving. He was probably fatally wounded, Brian told himself, and made no effort to go back for him.

Doors had been slamming open all around him. From the stairwell came a riotous tumult as roomers charged out of their rooms, first in response to the gunfire, and now to the ominous, terrifying smell of smoke. Men throughout the hotel began bellowing, "Fire!" After that came the screams of terrified wives and consorts.

Three of Brian's crew raced up the stairs, Lundstrom in the lead.

"You all right, Boss?" he asked, staring fearfully past him at the flames winking through the smoke.

"Yes, but Sim's still up there!"

"Jesus," the man said.

He pushed past Brian and hurried down the hallway, vanishing momentarily in the smoke's thick pall. A moment later he staggered back, wiping his streaming eyes.

"He aint there, Boss! He's gone!"

That was hard to believe, but Brian was in no position to deny it.

"Let's get out of here!"

Brian, Lundstrom, and the two others plunged back down the stairs, brushing ruthlessly past the hotel's lodgers. The rest of his crew was waiting nervously in the lobby, and as soon as Brian showed, they stampeded down the back hallway and out into the alley. A moment later, they were on their horses, galloping out of town.

One down, Brian told himself grimly. One more to go—that damned sodbuster, the man he'd thought he had killed. Unlike that crazy U.S. deputy, he'd be eager to deal. He'd have to deal now.

He felt bad about Sim, but there was nothing he could do about that now. He just wouldn't think about it.

Inside the blazing room, Longarm hefted the mattress off the bed and charged once more through the flames and out through the doorway, the flames licking at his britches. The choking clouds of smoke made it impossible for him to see Levinson and, he presumed, for Levinson to see him. His head down as he peered out from under the mattress, he started down the hallway and almost tripped headlong over the body of the man he had shot. Reaching down he grabbed him and pulled him along behind him a few feet, only to see the dim outline of the man he assumed was Brian Levinson standing at the head of the stairs with members of his crew. Longarm ducked into the abandoned room next to his, dragging the wounded man in after him, then throwing aside the mattress.

He closed the door. The smoke from his room had penetrated into this room as well, the wall between them already glowing. In a moment the flames would burst through, he realized. He hurried to the window and looked down. It was too far to jump. He went back to the door and pulled it open a crack to see one of Levinson's crew slip past it, crouching, his bandanna held up to his face as he hurried back to Levinson. Levinson and his men vanished down the stairs.

Longarm dragged the wounded man out of the room and hurried down the hall away from the flames, which by this time had leaped across the hallway and were licking hungrily at the door opposite. At the head of the stairs, he was joined by six frantic roomers, some half-dressed, others still in their nightgowns. Longarm flung the wounded man over his shoulder and joined the stampede plunging down the stairs to the lobby, the smoke following after them as near-hysterical cries came now from every floor.

Bursting out of the hotel, still carrying the Jinglebob cowhand, he crossed the street, picking his way through the aroused citizenry. By the time he reached the doc's office, a bucket brigade had been formed. He burst into the office with the wounded man. The doc was already awake, standing at the window, a bottle in his hand as he peered out at the excitement.

"In the back room," the doc told Longarm as soon as he saw the wounded man. "There's another cot in there."

Longarm carried his burden into the back room and flung him down onto the cot, grateful to be free of his weight. The doc followed after him, sat down on the cot beside the Jinglebob rider, and turned him over onto his back to examine his wound.

"Who's this?" the doc asked, using his thumb to lift back the unconscious man's eyelids. He rested the back of his hand against his throat.

"One of Levinson's cowhands."

The doc leaned back to take in all of the man's features. "Yes. I recognize him now. He's Sim Bond, the foreman."

As he spoke he pulled a sheet up over the man's face and stood up.

"Dead?" asked Longarm wearily.

"Yep. You could've saved yourself the trouble of haulin' him over here. That bullet was lodged just above the heart. He couldn't've lived more'n a few minutes after taking that hit. Who shot him?"

"I did. He and his boss came into my room, guns blazing."

"His boss? You mean Levinson?"

Longarm nodded.

"You're lucky to be alive."

"I know that, Doc."

Longarm walked into the doc's office and looked down at Sam Waller. "How's Sam?"

"Better."

Longarm bent over the sleeping wrangler. He did look better, at that. Glad for some good news at last, he joined the doc as they walked out onto the porch to watch the fire. It was clear by this time that little could be done to save the hotel. All the bucket brigade could hope to do was keep the fire from spreading to the tinder-dry roofs of adjacent buildings.

Longarm pulled a chair out of the doc's office and sat down to watch. He had been pulling on his boots when the kerosene lamp exploded on the floor in front of him; he had been able to save his vest and coat, his derringer, and the cross-draw rig. But his hat was long gone.

He looked at the doc. "You got a hat I could use?"

"Mine wouldn't fit, but I have a few left over from customers won't be needing headgear no more. There's a couple in the back might fit you."

"I'll take a look later," Longarm said, glancing down at his singed boots. He ran his hand through his hair and found to his surprise that patches of his thick hair had been singed clear to the scalp. He guessed he was lucky to be alive, at that.

As dawn lightened the eastern sky, it was clear that only one building would be lost in addition to the hotel: a small dress shop. Fortunately, the gunfire had awakened every hotel guest, and not a single one had been lost in the blaze. Walking along the sidewalk in a black Stetson he had selected from the doc's collection, Longarm noted how dismal the town of Pine Hill looked, what with the dress shop and the hotel a charred, stinking mess, and the jailhouse still not completely rebuilt.

He let himself into the sheriff's office, and before long the two who had volunteered to serve as deputies showed up. They looked completely done in, and Longarm realized they had been up most of the night fighting the hotel blaze. Longarm was impressed.

The oldest of the two, a gray-haired man in his late forties, introduced himself as Tex Loomis. His companion, a younger, lankier, darker version of Tex, called himself Concho, in keeping with the silver conches sewn into the hatband of his flat-crowned plainsman hat.

The two rode together, it appeared, and Tex, the oldest, appeared to be the spokesman for both. It was he who reminded Longarm that they'd be needing badges. Longarm found the badges Seth and Cal had left behind and tossed one to each of them. They pinned them on somewhat self-consciously, then stepped back nervously, adjusting their holstered revolvers as they did so.

"What now?" asked Tex.

"You two had time for breakfast?"

"Nope."

"I suggest we visit the restaurant. We can chart our course while we eat."

"Suits me," said Tex.

"Yeah, I could eat a bear," said Concho.

"And it'll be on me," Longarm told them.

"You don't need to do that," Tex said.

"Sure I do. I'm celebrating."

"Celebratin' what?"

"That I'll be eating a piece of steak, instead of being one," he said, clapping his hat on and brushing past them out the door.

· · ·

"Custis was right," Ruthanne called to Jim. "Look!"

The riders disgorging onto the flat were obviously Jinglebob hands; even from this distance Ruthanne recognized Brian from his peculiarly stiff, inflexible ride. Strung out behind him she counted seven more riders.

Ruthanne turned and hurried into the ranch house. Eben, his wife, and the two children were in the living room, two loaded rifles leaning against the wall beside them. She warned Jenny to keep the children quiet and not wake up her husband, then snatched up one of the rifles and rushed out onto the veranda.

By that time Jim had alerted the rest of the riders, who were already scattering to their positions, extra cartridge belts draped over their chests. Some were in the barn's loft, some in the bushes behind the bunkhouse, and a few were scrambling up into the oaks shading the compound. As soon as the men were properly deployed, Jim hurried up onto the porch.

"What are you doing with that rifle?" he asked Ruthanne.

"What do you think?"

"For God's sake, Ruthanne, get inside."

"*You* should get inside. You've only got one arm."

He ducked his head and flung off the sling supporting his left arm. "I only need one hand to shoot with."

She put her hand on his arm. "Perhaps we won't have to," she said. "I know Brian."

"You think you know him. He's come for Eben, as Long warned us he might. We aren't going to let him, are we?"

"Of course not."

"I wish you'd stay inside."

"Why is it so important, Jim?"

"Dammit, you know why."

"There's no reason for you to curse."

"I'm sorry. I didn't mean that. It just came out."

"Besides, I guess I do know why."

He looked at her for a long moment, a smile breaking across his face; she felt her heart soar.

"Be careful."

He nodded, ducked back off the porch, and hurried out to meet the oncoming riders.

Thompson planted himself firmly in the path of Levinson and his men. Levinson pulled up. The rest of his weary riders came to a halt beside him, the dust raised by the horses' hooves obscuring them. Brian squinted down at Thompson.

"No need for you to be carrying that weapon, Jim," Levinson chided.

"What do want, Mr. Levinson?"

"I want to talk to Eben Heath."

"The man you tried to kill?"

"I shot Eben in self-defense. He had a loaded shotgun. He'd already let go one barrel at me."

"Now, why do you suppose he did that, Mr. Levinson?"

"Get out of my way, Jim. I'm coming through this gate. Eben's in there, and I want to talk to him. I've got a deal for him."

"What kind of a deal? A bellyful of lead?"

"I didn't ride out here to argue with you, Jim. It's Eben I want to see. Let me through so I can talk to him."

"He's in no condition to talk to you, Mr. Levinson. Besides, I don't think he'd be interested."

"Goddammit, Jim! You let me be the judge of that!"

As he started to spur his horse past Thompson, a rifle cracked from high in one of the oaks, the round digging up a chunk of dirt just in front of Brian's horse. The horse shied back so quickly, it almost unhorsed Brian. Brian swore, clung to the saddle, and gentled the horse, his face black with fury.

"You'll regret this, Jim!"

"I'd regret it a whole lot more if I let you and your men into this compound. I suggest you pull out. Now."

Levinson hesitated a moment, his anger palpable, then wheeled his horse and led his riders back toward the flat. Thompson watched them go for a minute or two, then started back to the ranch house, keeping his eye on them as he walked. Just above the stream, Brian pulled his mount around and head down, led the charge back to the gate. They swept through it, guns blazing.

Thompson flung himself to one side and fired up futilely at the riders pounding past. From all sides Circle T riders opened up on the horsemen, but they swept on toward the house unscathed. Furious, Thompson jumped up and raced after them, firing at the riders. As Brian leaped from his horse and plunged into the house, the rest of his men rode around to the back, while others circled the bunkhouse and blacksmith's shack, the gunfire almost continuous.

Inside the house, before she could aim her rifle, Ruthanne was shoved brutally aside, the rifle torn from her grasp as Levinson stormed past her into the living room. Jenny had planted herself in front of the sofa where her husband lay, her two children cowering behind her. Eben was awake, a revolver in his hand, its bore pointed straight up at Levinson's belly.

"You come a step closer and I'll pull this trigger," he warned, his voice faint, almost feeble.

Levinson smiled. "I came here to apologize, Eben, and your friends try to kill me. That ain't nice."

"Apologize!" Ruthanne cried, storming up beside him. "How dare you come in here like this, Brian!"

Brian pushed her roughly aside, turned back to Eben, and in the same motion snatched the revolver out of Eben's hand. Sticking it into his belt, he said to the man, "Think it over. I'll rebuild your barn. The spur line will go around your homestead. How's that?"

"And I forget you tried to kill me."

"That was a mistake. But don't forget. You shot

first with that cannon you were carrying."

"You mean I was supposed to stand there and let you burn down my barn?"

"Let bygones be bygones."

At that moment, Jim Thompson charged in. Ruthanne met him and kept him from raising his gun.

"Damn you, Levinson," Jim spat.

Turning back to Eben, Levinson said, "I got some news for you. If you think that deputy marshal is going to help you, forget it. He died last night in a hotel fire. A terrible thing."

Ruthanne gasped at the news. Eben looked with dismay at his wife. Noting this reaction, Levinson was pleased. No doubt about it. The nester had been banking heavily on the lawman.

"Well?" Levinson prodded. "What's it going to be? Your wife a widower, or you get a nice new barn filled with fodder and no more trouble from the Jinglebob or the Grand Northern?"

"You threatening me?"

"Now, how can you say that? But you know how things can happen. You go out to check a fence and don't come back. Maybe you get into a brawl in town, get your head bashed in. Lots of terrible things can happen."

Eben had no choice and he realized it. He glanced up at his wife. There were tears on her cheeks. Beaten, he nodded to Levinson.

"But I'm warning you, Levinson, if you or any of your hirelings ever strays onto my land, I'll shoot them down."

162

"Harsh words," Levinson chided. "Harsh words. But I understand how you feel. I'm glad you got the sense to see things realistically."

"Get out of my house," Ruthanne said, seething.

"Yes, ma'am," Levinson said, touching his hat brim to her.

He turned then and strode out onto the veranda, dropping Eben's Colt on a chair by the door as he went out. The gunfire outside had come to a halt when everyone saw that Levinson had made it into the house. Now, as he descended the veranda steps and gathered up his horse's reins, the rest of his riders rode out of cover to join him.

Before long Levinson and his men were riding out through the gate on the way back to the Jinglebob. Standing on the veranda beside Jim Thompson, Ruthanne wept with shame that she had ever been gentle with such a man.

Chapter 10

Without waiting for Longarm to reach the ranch house, Ruthanne ran down the veranda steps to greet him.

"Longarm!" she cried. "We thought you were dead!"

"A slight exaggeration," he told her, dismounting.

Longarm's two deputies dismounted also. He introduced them to Ruthanne, who eagerly invited them in to the ranch house for a glass of her famous lemonade. Tex and Concho solemnly thanked her. Jim Thompson, his left arm in a sling, hurried over to join them, obviously as surprised and delighted as Ruthanne.

"I think I can guess who brought you the

good news," Longarm commented grimly as they started for the ranchhouse.

"Brian Levinson," Jim Thompson told him. "He came riding in like you said he might. He said you had perished in a hotel fire."

"Wasn't there a fire?" Ruthanne asked Longarm.

"Oh, there was a fire, all right. The hotel's a smoldering mess right now. And I got singed some—but I managed to escape in time. Levinson's foreman was not so lucky."

"Sim Bond?"

Longarm described it all then. Finishing up, he said, "I assume when Levinson showed up here, you weren't quite able to drive him off."

"We tried to," Jim admitted. "A lot of lead flew, but it didn't do any good. Fortunately, only one man got winged, and he's all right now."

"Brian forced his way into the house," Ruthanne said. "And after he told Eben you were dead, he made Eben promise not to press charges against him."

Longarm shook his head in grudging admiration. "He might have gotten away with it if I *had* died in that fire. Let me talk to Eben. How is he, by the way? Did this business shake him up any?"

"He'll be glad to see you," Ruthanne assured Longarm, "no matter how shook-up he might be."

As a matter of fact, Eben looked a lot better than he had the last time Longarm saw him. When Longarm strode in Eben's drawn face lit up like a lamp.

"So that's what the commotion out there was all about," he said.

"Back from the dead," Longarm said, nodding.

Jenny appeared in the kitchen doorway, eyes wide in astonishment, as pleased as her husband to see Longarm standing there. Her toddler peeked out from behind her skirts. "But Brian said you were dead!"

Ruthanne smiled over at her. "Looks like he was counting his chickens before they hatched."

Longarm looked down at Eben. "You still think you have to keep that deal you made with Levinson?"

"Not on your life."

"Then you'll testify against him?"

"As soon as I'm able."

Longarm looked at Ruthanne. "How far behind Levinson am I?"

"He left about a half hour ago."

"Good. Maybe we can catch up to him. I'd like to get him before he reaches the Jinglebob."

"Oh?"

"Thing is, I don't want to tangle with his mother. She reminds me of an angry wasp."

"You ain't goin' after him alone, are you?" Jim Thompson asked.

"Nope. Wouldn't think of it. I got Tex and Concho here to side me. Should be a cakewalk. I got a badge and the town council's authority behind me."

"You think that'll be enough?"

"It will have to be." Longarm glanced at his

two deputies, who were still moistening their lips in anticipation of that lemonade Ruthanne had promised them. "Let's go, men."

As they got ready to mount up a moment later, Concho muttered, "I sure would've liked some of that lemonade she promised."

"Me too," said Tex. "Maybe laced with a little something extra."

"Forget it," Longarm said to them both. "When this is done, I'll buy you both a barrel of lemonade each."

The two deputies grinned sheepishly and swung into their saddles. A moment later they rode out of the compound, spanking leather.

Dutch chucked his hat back off his forehead and, leaning on his saddlehorn, gazed down through the trees at the big house.

"Quiet, ain't it," he muttered to Studs.

"Levinson's off somewhere, I reckon," said Studs, chewing on a grass stem. "Up to no good, more than likely."

"I figure we'll just go down there and wait for him."

"Good idea."

"Another thing. Why don't we up that bonus he promised us?"

"I been thinkin' the same thing."

"How's two thousand apiece sound to you?"

"More. Look at that house. And he owns a bank, for Christ's sake. And think of poor Gimpy."

"Yeah. I say five thousand apiece."

"That's more like it."

"He's going to protest."

"Hope he does, the bastard. Then we can cut out his gizzard and go take it from his bank all by ourselves."

"Yeah," said Dutch. "I'd like that."

He nudged his horse down the slope and on through the oaks, coming at the big house from the rear. They dismounted while still in the trees and headed for the small back porch. As they neared it, a huge Indian housekeeper stepped out onto it, carrying a load of wash in a wicker basket.

She froze on the porch, watching them approach. When they started for her, she put down the bucket and reached back for the door.

"Just hold it right there," Dutch told her softly, his big Colt seeming to jump into his right hand.

"We just come for a visit," said Studs. "No need for you to get all upset."

Behind them a calm voice said, "You put down guns."

Without holstering their weapons, Dutch and Studs turned slowly. A small Indian with long pigtails and a Stetson with a red feather in it was holding a Winchester on them.

"You put down guns," the Indian repeated.

"We just want to talk to your boss," Dutch explained patiently.

"Boss ain't here."

The big housekeeper fled back into the house,

and a moment later a woman in a wheelchair appeared in the open doorway, a shotgun on her lap.

"It's all right, Juan," she said. "I'll handle this."

Reluctantly, the Indian lowered his Winchester and walked back toward the bunkhouse.

Dutch turned about to peer at the old woman and the shotgun she was holding. Slowly he dropped his sixgun back into its holster. Studs did the same.

"Now, what was it you gents wanted to see Brian about?" the woman asked coldly.

"He owes us," said Dutch.

"You the men he brung up from Texas?"

"What's left of us."

"We lost a man since," said Studs.

"I see. Then this is a business visit."

"Sure," said Dutch.

"You usually come on a house like this, at the back with drawn guns?"

"It seemed like the sensible thing to do," explained Dutch, "considering."

"Considering what?"

"Hey, lady," said Studs, "you goin' to make us stand out here like this in the hot sun? After your boy brung us all the way up here from Texas?"

She looked at him shrewdly, then nudged her wheelchair back out of the doorway. "Come in," she said. "I'll have the housekeeper bring you some lemonade."

"We're hungry too," said Studs, following Dutch up onto the back porch and shoving the basket of wash aside with his foot. "We ain't had breakfast yet."

"Anything you want—within reason—Carlotta can prepare for you."

"That's right nice of you," said Dutch, taking off his hat as he stepped into the kitchen.

"Follow me," the old woman said, guiding her wheelchair across the kitchen and down a long hallway.

She led them into a cool living room, spun her wheelchair about, and with the shotgun still resting on her lap, indicated a sofa and an upholstered morris chair they could use. She called out to Carlotta, who hurried in promptly. She told the big woman the men were hungry and would like some breakfast.

"Flapjacks and steak," Studs told Carlotta.

"And doughnuts," Dutch said. "I smelled them when I came in."

The Indian disappeared from the doorway.

"Now," said Brian's mother. "What's this all about? If Brian hired you, why hasn't he paid you—and how is it you showed up here in this fashion?"

"He double-crossed us," Dutch said simply.

"You want to explain that?"

"He sicked a posse on us while we was at his line shack and lit out before they got there."

"I see. You're sure of this, are you?"

"Sure enough."

"But you managed to elude the posse and now—like two bad pennies—you've shown up here."

171

"Only to get what's due us," Studs reminded her.

"And just how much might that be?"

"We figure five thousand apiece," said Dutch.

"Isn't that rather steep?"

"That's what we want."

"On what sum did you and my son settle?"

"A thousand each."

"Then that is all you shall get. A thousand each."

Dutch smiled at the old harpy, then looked around at Studs. "You think that'll be all right, Studs?"

"I guess what has to be has to be," the young man said philosophically, "long as she throws in a good breakfast."

The smell of pancakes, bacon, and coffee coming from the kitchen was almost overpowering. Dutch felt his mouth watering.

"Go into the kitchen and get your breakfast," Brian's mother said. "You'll have to eat alone. I can't stand to watch men eat."

"Sure," said Studs, getting to his feet.

Dutch followed after Studs. As he left the living room, he glanced back to see the old bitch watching them go, her eyes gleaming like a vulture settling beside a rotting carcass. He shuddered and followed Studs out into the kitchen, where the best-looking breakfast in his life had been set out for them on the big round kitchen table.

Each man grabbed a chair and brought it over to the table, then scooted up closer.

"Man, oh, man" said Studs, rubbing his palms together. "Ain't this something!"

"Sure is," said Dutch, stabbing the pile of pancakes with his fork. "Makes me think of Gimpy. He could make a breakfast like this if you gave him the makin's."

He grabbed the pitcher of syrup and poured it liberally over his stack of pancakes, then began slicing them crosswise so as to get the syrup down in between them. Then he dumped half of the bacon onto his plate and grabbed two thick slabs of buttered toast off a plate beside him.

Both men began eating greedily, hungrily, their teeth chomping down joyously on the light, feathery pancakes, the crisp bacon crunching loudly. They made so much noise as they stuffed the food in, breathing heavily, almost grunting like pigs at a feeding trough—there was no way they could hear the wheels of Clara's wheelchair as she rolled swiftly down the hallway toward them.

As she swept into the kitchen, she lifted her shotgun and fired a barrel at Studs, the blast so deafening the kitchen's walls seemed to expand outward. Reeling back in horror and surprise, Carlotta slipped and went down heavily. The buckshot caught Studs in his left side, cutting him nearly in half and flinging his mangled body onto Dutch's lap, the force of which knocked Dutch sideways off his chair.

He landed on his back, his Colt jumping into his hand. His head struck the floor hard. But it was not hard enough to knock him out. The Indian

173

housekeeper, scrambling to her feet, slammed out the kitchen door and pounded away from the house. Peering out from under the table, Dutch could see Levinson's mother pumping her arms furiously as she drove the wheelchair backward, then around the table to get a clear shot at him. He flung himself under the table and fired up at her. The bullet whined past her head and took out a kitchen window. She poked the shotgun down at him, but before she could aim properly, he reached out from under the table and grabbed the barrel, thrusting it aside just as it went off. The detonation nearly blew out his eardrums, but he clung to the weapon and yanked it out of her frail, murderous hands. She cried out, in a veritable fury at being thwarted.

He scrambled out from under the table and towering over her, clubbed her with the barrel of his gun, striking her about the head and shoulders, consumed by a mindless fury, as if he were stomping on a scorpion he had discovered in his sleeping bag. When at last he got hold of himself, he pulled back, panting, sweat pouring down his face. The old harpy was slumped back in the wheelchair, her eyes closed, one eyebrow lost, great welts swelling on her parchment face. Her mouth was a crushed, ruby hole with tiny bits of teeth flecking the broken lips. On the front of her dress, from a gaping wound in her neck, a steady trickle of blood began to flow.

He was startled by the sound of rapid hoofbeats. He peered through the shattered windowpane and

saw the Indian and the housekeeper on separate
mounts galloping full tilt into the hills back of the
ranch. He left the window, grabbed the wheelchair's handles, and ran the old bitch back into
the living room. Turning her chair around, he
left her in a corner near the window, dropped
the empty shotgun onto her lap, and went back
to the kitchen.

"Studs?" he cried, kneeling beside him to cradle
his head in his arms. "Studs!"

There was no response. Inspecting the gaping
hole in his partner's side, the gleaming white
shards of bone, the exposed, shattered organs,
he realized there never would be. He felt sick,
his senses reeling as he looked around him past
the overturned chairs, noting the wreckage of the
breakfast she had offered them. Broken flapjacks
were scattered over the floor; the syrup flowing
from the broken pitcher was already mixing with
Studs's blood.

He got to his feet. Who would've thought that
old witch would do such a thing?

He heard the clatter of horses entering the compound, and ran down the hallway into the living
room to peer out the window. Levinson was back,
his crew with him. As Dutch watched, he heard
Levinson tell his men to move out as soon as they
could. Most of their stock had run off into the
hills. Grumbling some, the men headed for the
cookshack for coffee.

This meant the Jinglebob's cook must have
been off riding with the rest of Levinson's hands.

A break for him, Dutch realized. He took out his Colt and sat down in a chair just inside the entrance to the living room. In a few minutes, he heard Levinson's heavy boots on the veranda steps. A second later the door was pushed open. In full stride, Levinson passed the living room, then paused and backed up to peer in.

Dutch waggled his Colt at him. "Come on in, Boss Man," he said. "We been waiting for you."

Levinson stepped in and stared across the room at his mother. She looked worse than she had when Dutch had wheeled her in. A growing pool of blood was spreading under her wheelchair.

"Ma!" Levinson cried.

He started to rush past Dutch, but Dutch stood up and jammed his Colt into Levinson's side.

"Hold it right there and keep your voice down," Dutch told him, lifting Levinson's Colt from his holster and tossing it into a corner.

Levinson held up, his frantic eyes still on his mother's slumped figure. "My God! Look at her! What'd you do to her, you bastard!"

"What'd I do to *her*?" Dutch snarled. "It's what she done to Studs and tried to do to me. She just got through cutting him in half with that shotgun."

"Is . . . is she dead?"

"Pretty damn close to it, I'd say. Sorry. But she didn't give me any choice."

"Dammnit, let me go to her!" Levinson cried.

He started for his mother then, and Dutch stepped back to let him go. Sobbing, Levinson fell on his knees before his mother and flung his arms around her tiny figure, clutching her distractedly to him, calling for her over and over again.

The man's obvious grief left Dutch completely unmoved. She was a harpy and had killed Studs in cold blood. He still trembled with indignation when he thought of how she had done it. Watching closely, he kept his Colt leveled on them both.

His plan was to stay in the ranch house with them until the crew rode out. Intent on getting what he had come for, he was in no hurry. The way he saw it, Levinson probably kept a sizable amount of cash in a safe somewhere in the house, and Dutch wasn't going back to Texas a poor man—not after what this bastard had led him into.

His attention was caught suddenly by hoofbeats approaching the ranch house. He hurried over to the window and saw that damned U.S. deputy, a star pinned to his shirt, and two deputies getting ready to dismount. He turned away from the window just as Levinson flung himself away from his mother. The old bat was sitting upright in the wheelchair, her eyes blazing, the shotgun he had left in her lap aimed at him. As he started to fling up his Colt to cut her down, both barrels thundered. He felt himself being flung violently back through the doorway. A numbing red haze blotted out the room. Coughing violently, unable to breathe, he reached up to his throat, but found it had turned to mush, and fell backward into oblivion.

The moment he heard the shotgun blast, Longarm ran for the steps, dashed up them, stormed into the house, and found himself staring down at a man whose head had nearly been blown clear off his body. Beyond that, in the kitchen he saw the sprawled, bloody mess of another shotgun victim.

He turned.

Standing beside his mother's wheelchair, Levinson raised his sixgun and fired at Longarm. The bullet nicked Longarm high on his left shoulder and slammed him back against the wall. He kept on his feet, however, and fired back repeatedly, each bullet finding its mark. Levinson crumpled to the floor.

Longarm walked into the living room and saw that Levinson's mother, beaten almost to a pulp, was slowly, doggedly, inserting two fresh charges into her shotgun.

Gently, he took the weapon from her.

Chapter 11

Longarm swung down from the train and glanced
around the platform. He had been away more
than a week in all, and he was returning without
the man he had gone after, so he was not at all
surprised that Billy wasn't there to greet him. As
a matter of fact, he was glad he wasn't. He had
planted a seed with that telegram he had sent to
Billy, and what he wanted now was to find out if
it had borne any fruit.

He strode through the crowd, reached the street
outside, and hailed a hack. Dropping his carpetbag on the seat beside him, he gave the driver
the name of a saloon on Wykoop Street. When
he reached it, he strode inside and found himself
an empty booth. Slipping into it, he dropped his

carpetbag beside him and brushed some of the train's soot from his person. A girl came over to take his order. He ordered a bottle of Maryland rye. When it came, he paid her, filled his glass, and leaned back to enjoy it.

An overpainted bar girl with a pile of auburn hair, pearl earrings, and at least a pound of pearl necklaces appeared beside his booth. She cocked her head and moistened her rouged lips with the tip of her tongue.

"Custis?"

He knew he should recognize her, and she was vaguely familiar, but he couldn't remember her name. "Hi, Pearl," he said, taking a wild guess.

"You remembered!"

"I never forget a pretty face."

"That ain't all I got that's pretty."

"I know that, love."

"May I join you?"

"Nothing ever stopped you before."

"And nothing ever made you say no, either." She sat down next to him and moved as close to him as she could get without slipping into his Levi's. "Course, I ain't seen you in a long time— maybe a year or so."

"Oh, yeah. I remember."

"There was all that excitement, remember?"

"You mean about that kid? The one who got shot running by the saloon?"

She nodded and looked at his drink. When he started to push the bottle toward her, she shook her head. "I'll just have a beer. Do you mind?"

"Suit yourself."

Longarm waved over a girl and asked for a beer.

"I mean I don't like nothin' real hard to drink this early in the day."

"That's all right, Pearl. I won't spank you."

"I wish you would," she said teasingly, her hand dropping to his thigh and squeezing it.

"It's too early for that too, Pearl."

She shrugged, then smiled at him. "Okay, just trying."

"You remember that fellow I collared in here— the one who shot that kid by mistake? That kid we were just talking about."

"Oh, him! He's not my type, Custis. He's a real loser. But there's one thing I can't understand."

"What's that, Pearl?"

"Why'd you let him out of jail so soon?"

"We didn't let him out. He broke free of the constable after he was sentenced."

"Oh," she said, shrugging. "I didn't know that. He said he was a free man. That no one was after him."

"Who said?"

"Flem."

Longarm looked quickly around the saloon. It was early and there was very little smoke to obscure his vision. If Flem Cutter was in this saloon at that moment, Longarm could not see him. He leaned forward and smiled at Pearl.

"Now let me hear that again, Pearl. You just

said that Flem said no one was after him. That right?"

She nodded solemnly, aware that Longarm was no longer in a kidding mood. "That's what he told me, Custis."

"That means you've seen him around here lately."

"Sure."

Longarm took another judicious sip of his whiskey. This was almost too good to be true—but then, as he recalled, Flem Cutter was not the brightest of men.

"Do you expect him in tonight?"

"Oh, he's here now."

"That so?"

"He's upstairs with Kitty." She smiled. "He's having a matinee. He likes to get an early start."

"Say, I remember Kitty. You think she'd see me next?"

"Custis! What's wrong with me?"

"For you and me, its better in the night. Know what I mean? More romantic."

"Well, I guess that's all right. As a matter of fact, I'm not eager myself. I got my monthly visitor—thank God."

Longarm patted her arm, got to his feet, and finished his drink. "Can you take me up to Kitty?"

She got up uncertainly. "You want me to take you up there now? Kitty's probably not finished yet. Flem is real slow."

"That's okay."

"You're sure in a hurry."

"Let's go."

"Boy, what's Kitty got?"

"Flem Cutter."

She frowned, not getting at all what he meant by that, then moved ahead of him across the saloon. He let her lead the way through a door opening onto a narrow stairway, and kept behind her as they mounted the stairs to the second floor. As they walked along the second-floor landing, Longarm found himself approaching Flem Cutter. The man had obviously just left Kitty's crib and was walking with his head down, buttoning his fly. Longarm let Pearl move past Flem down the hallway as he planted himself in front of the fugitive.

"Hello, Flem," Longarm said.

As he glanced up, Flem's mouth dropped open. "Longarm!"

"It's me, all right."

Longarm snapped a cuff around Flem's wrist.

"Hey, you can't take me in! I was burned to death up in Pine Hill, Wyoming."

"It was all a terrible mistake, Flem."

"I'm legally dead! I read it in the paper."

"You shouldn't believe everything you read in the papers, Flem. Come along."

"Custis!" Pearl called. "Here's Kitty!"

Pearl was standing at the end of the hall, a small, perky little blond standing beside her.

"Later, Pearl."

"But what about Kitty?"

183

Longarm threw them both a kiss, closed the other cuff around his left wrist, and hauled Flem Cutter down the stairs after him.

Billy Vail smiled and shook his head admiringly. "So that's why that telegram said Flem Cutter had died in the blaze."

Longarm nodded. "I knew the dead outlaw wasn't Flem, but I was hoping the story that he was dead would get out."

It was later the same day in Longarm's favorite watering hole, the lounge at the Windsor Hotel. He had plans to visit a certain society gal up on Sherman Avenue that night, but wanted first to explain matters thoroughly to Billy Vail.

"And you figured it would flush the bastard," Vail said.

"Right. I never did find it easy to believe Cutter would go all the way to Wyoming in the first place."

Longarm took a badge out of his pocket and placed it down beside Vail's glass.

"What's this?" Vail asked, picking it up.

"A dead man's badge. Belonged to Sheriff Tompkins. I wore it for a while. It's yours if you want it."

"Yeah, thanks, Longarm. Much obliged." He polished it a bit, stared at it thoughtfully for a moment, then pocketed it. "You say that ranch foreman is running for sheriff now?"

"You mean Jim Thompson? Yeah. I think he'll get elected too. It has something to do with him wanting to court the lady who owns the ranch. It'll be easier for him if he's not in her employ, you see."

"And easier for her too."

"Precisely."

"What I can't understand, Longarm, is why Levinson started blazing away at you in his ranch house."

"They way I figure it, when I turned up alive, he knew Eben Heath would testify against him. That meant it was all over for him—and it had something to do with his mother too. He thought she was dying. They had a strange relationship, from all I heard. Not a very pleasant one. But he couldn't see himself going on without her. He just didn't care anymore."

Vail took a sip of his beer and wiped off his mouth with the back of his hand. He smiled sardonically and shook his head. "And yet she outlived him—after a beating like that."

"Outlived both of her sons, Billy, and had them buried where she couldn't find them, somewhere on her land without markers. It was as if they had never existed."

"You mean as if she had never *wanted* them to exist."

"That's right."

Vail shook his head.

"She was a tough, stringy old bird. I'm glad it was them two gunslicks who had to deal with her, not me."

"So am I, Longarm."

A woman in black, her hair a dark red, her eyes a flashing emerald, her mouth a slash of pouting lips, appeared beside the booth. She smiled first at Billy Vail, who almost began to drool openly, then slipped into the booth beside Longarm, her silken form warm against his.

"You're back at last, Custis," she purred.

"Hi, Randy."

"Is that all you have to say to me—after all this time?"

"That's just for openers."

"Were you going anywhere special tonight?"

He thought of that society gal up on Sherman Avenue. She had more class, maybe—but not nearly as much enthusiasm.

"No," he said, "not really."

"That's nice. Did you know I've taken a room in this hotel?"

"No, as a matter of fact, I didn't."

"It'll be so much more convenient for us." She smiled across at Billy. "You're cute, Marshal Vail. And I've heard so much about you. Would you like me to introduce you to a friend of mine?"

"I couldn't afford it," Billy said, hastily, finishing his beer.

As he left the booth, he bid Randy good night, then looked back at Longarm. "I want you in before noon, Longarm—the latest."

"Thanks, Billy,"

Longarm leaned back in the booth, one arm snaking around Randy's waist, Randy's hand moving elsewhere.

Watch for

LONGARM AND THE KILLER'S SHADOW

145th novel in the bold LONGARM series
from Jove

Coming in January!

A special offer for people who enjoy reading the best Westerns published today. If you enjoyed this book, subscribe now and get . . .

TWO FREE WESTERNS!
A $5.90 VALUE—NO OBLIGATION

If you enjoyed this book and would like to read more of the very best Westerns being published today, you'll want to subscribe to True Value's Western Home Subscription Service. If you enjoyed the book you just read and want more of the most exciting, adventurous, action packed Westerns, subscribe now.

TWO FREE BOOKS

When you subscribe, we'll send you your first month's shipment of the newest and best 6 Westerns for you to preview. With your first shipment, two of these books will be yours as our introductory gift to you absolutely FREE, regardless of what you decide to do.

Special Subscriber Savings

As a True Value subscriber all regular monthly selections will be billed at the low subscriber price of just $2.45 each. That's at least a savings of $3.00 each month below the publishers price. There is never any shipping, handling or other hidden charges. What's more there is no minimum number of books you must buy, you may return any selection for full credit and you can cancel your subscription at any time. A TRUE VALUE!

Mail the coupon below

To start your subscription and receive 2 FREE WESTERNS, fill out the coupon below and mail it today. We'll send your first shipment which includes 2 FREE BOOKS as soon as we receive it.

Mail To: True Value Home Subscription Services, Inc.
P.O. Box 5235
120 Brighton Road
Clifton, New Jersey 07015-5235

YES! I want to start receiving the very best Westerns being published today. Send me my first shipment of 6 Westerns for me to preview FREE for 10 days. If I decide to keep them, I'll pay for just 4 of the books at the low subscriber price of $2.45 each; a total of $9.80 (a $17.70 value). Then each month I'll receive the 6 newest and best Westerns to preview Free for 10 days. If I'm not satisfied I may return them within 10 days and owe nothing. Otherwise I'll be billed at the special low subscriber rate of $2.45 each; a total of $14.70 (at least a $17.70 value) and save $3.00 off the publishers price. There are never any shipping, handling or other hidden charges. I understand I am under no obligation to purchase any number of books and I can cancel my subscription at any time, no questions asked. In any case the 2 FREE books are mine to keep.

Name _____

Address _____ Apt. # _____

City _____ State _____ Zip _____

Telephone # _____

Signature _____
(if under 18 parent or guardian must sign)
Terms and prices subject to change. Orders subject to acceptance by True Value Home Subscription Services, Inc.
